# CONCRETE KILLA 2

# Kingpen

**Lock Down Publications and Ca$h Presents**

# Concrete Killa 2
**A Novel by *Kingpen***

# Kingpen

**Lock Down Publications**
P.O. Box 944
Stockbridge, Ga 30281
www.lockdownpublications.com

Copyright 2021 Kingpen
Concrete Killa 2

**Lock Down Publications**
**Like our page on Facebook: Lock Down Publications**
**@**
www.facebook.com/lockdownpublications.ldp
Cover design and layout by: **Dynasty Cover Me**
Book interior design by: **Shawn Walker**
Edited by: **Nuel Uyi**

## Stay Connected with Us!

Text **LOCKDOWN** to 22828 to stay up-to-date with new releases, sneak peaks, contests and more...

Thank you!

# Submission Guideline.

Submit the first three chapters of your completed manuscript to ldpsubmissions@gmail.com, subject line: Your book's title. The manuscript must be in a .doc file and sent as an attachment. Document should be in Times New Roman, double spaced and in size 12 font. Also, provide your synopsis and full contact information. If sending multiple submissions, they must each be in a separate email.

Have a story but no way to send it electronically? You can still submit to LDP/Ca$h Presents. Send in the first three chapters, written or typed, of your completed manuscript to:

LDP: Submissions Dept
P.O. Box 944
Stockbridge, Ga 30281

*DO NOT send original manuscript. Must be a duplicate.*

Provide your synopsis and a cover letter containing your full contact information.

Thanks for considering LDP and Ca$h Presents.

## Dedication

I want to dedicate this to every man and woman who has lost their lives in the system. Once we're here, we're out of sight, out of mind. But, I'll never forget y'all! Rest in peace Vu, and 2-forty shorty. Y'all are finally free!

Joshua Kirby #2003156 Beto Unit
1391 F.M. 3328 Tennessee Colony, Tx 75880

# Kingpen

# Chapter 1

### Eastwood

"*I can't believe Hotboy left without me*," I thought to myself as I rushed to grab my shower materials. I then ran back upstairs to make sure Los and Lil' Chris were good. Peeping inside the cell, Los was still going hot and steamy with Saucadena. Lil' Chris even joined back in on the fun. I contemplated skipping my shower. I ain't gon' lie, I wanted another shot of that good Mexican pussy. I couldn't take a chance, though. Neither one of us had a condom. So, once I busted my nut, I'd be a damn fool to go behind another nigga without strapping up first. To me, that was som' gay shit.

I ran back downstairs once I made sure Los and Chris were okay. The C.O. on the keys gave me a hard time when I asked him to let me off the wing to take a shower. Hesitantly, he opened the gate to let me off the wing.

I walked swiftly to the shower. Hotboy had another thing coming once I saw him. His bitch ass had the nerve to leave me. I always waited on him.

The shower was empty, considering how many people usually showered at this time. I looked around for Hotboy. He was nowhere in sight. I figured he was probably already under the water.

I stripped and placed my clothes on the concrete slab. I tucked my shoes under my clothes and placed my towel over everything. I had to hide it because niggas would steal anything that they had a chance to steal, if given the opportunity.

Walking to the shower area, I looked around for Hotboy. He normally showered on the cold-water side. This time, he wasn't on that side. I finally spotted him a few feet away on the hot water side. He was in the far-right corner of the shower. He had this grin on his face, like he knew I'd been looking for him. Just as I stepped in the hot water section, three inmates crept towards Hotboy. The looks on their faces showed a portentous sign that they were out to kill. One of them held a shank.

The one with the shank reared back and came forward—full force. Everything happened so fast. All I could do to warn him was, scream: "Hotboy, watch out!"

***

**Hotboy**

I laughed to myself as I lowered my head under the water. I could tell Eastwood was in his feelings. We always waited on each other when it was time to hit the hallway. We did that just in case the laws would start tripping. The laws were known for jumping you, if they ever caught you by yourself. Me and Eastwood felt two people had a better chance at surviving than one. I rubbed my hands through my hair to wash the shampoo out. I heard footsteps approach, then I heard Eastwoods's voice.

"Hotboy, watch out!" Eastwood screamed.

I felt something sharp go through my side. The sudden impact caused me to fall to the floor. The shampoo blinded me, as I tried to open my eyes. Before I could see who my attacker was, a fist smashed into my face. I saw stars, then the room fell silent.

At first, I thought it was only one attacker, until I felt another pair of hands, then another. I tried to open my eyes, but the shampoo burned my eyes every time I tried to open them. I tried my best to fight back. It was pointless. I couldn't hit what I couldn't see. Then I felt another sharp pain go through my left side. Whoever my attackers were, they were bent on killing me. *But why?* I wondered. I didn't want to die in prison—especially not here, not like this. Naked, on this nasty shower floor.

"Lord, please, have mercy on me," I silently prayed. I used one hand to try my best to block the blows that were raining down on my head. I used my free hand to scoop some water from the shower floor to clean the shampoo from my eyes. I didn't care that the water was dirty. I was just trying to stay alive.

The water did its purpose. I looked up with blurred vision. Two inmates threw blow after blow at me. Out of my peripheral, I saw Eastwood going at it with a third inmate. Eastwood was beating his ass, but the inmate just wouldn't go down.

Eastwood caught him with a left hook, dropping him where he stood. Before his body could hit the ground, Eastwood ran to my rescue. He grabbed another inmate from behind, placing him in a chokehold.

"Dame!" the inmate grumbled.

The inmate that held the shank looked over his shoulder to his homie. In that brief second, I had to choose between life and death. I chose to live! I pushed myself off the ground, like I had a spring inside of me. As soon as I jumped up, Dame faced me again, but not fast enough. I was on him like a tiger does its prey. Dame swung the shank in a hook- like motion. Weaving the shank, I punched him in his ribs, knocking the wind out of him. I was a skilled boxer. Had been since the age of ten. People always respected me, so I never really had to showcase my skills, until now.

Dame recovered and bounced around from foot to foot. He tossed his shank from hand to hand, like they do in the movies. I looked over his shoulder to Eastwood as he crept up behind Dame. I shook my head at Eastwood. I didn't want any help; I wanted Dame all to myself.

Dame must've felt something. He rushed me, screaming "Ahhhhh!" to the top of his lungs.

He rushed me fast, cornering me, forcing my back against the shower wall. The way he held the shank, I had two options: Let him stab me again—so that I could get him close enough to relieve him of the shank—or, let him kill me.

As soon as he got within reach, I took a step forward, and braced myself. He did as expected. He jabbed the shank under my pecs. As soon as the shank touched my skin, I sidestepped him, while throwing an overhand at the same time. My timing was perfect. My fist landed dead center on his nose.

The shank fell from his hand, and he clutched the bridge of his nose. Blood spewed out as he cried like a bitch. Eastwood rushed to pick the shank up. My chest was hurting bad from the cut Dame had just put on me. My breathing got heavy. The room started spinning. I fell down to one knee and clutched my chest.

## Chapter 2

### Newton

"Hey, babe, are you ready to go?" Seth asked, as I sat in my wheelchair.

The doctor had finally signed my release papers to go home. I couldn't wait to finally be able to sleep in my own bed. The doctor gave me one requirement: attend an outpatient therapeutic treatment center.

"Most definitely!" I answered, thinking about everything that I have been missing since the incident: A good home cooked meal; watching Jacob run around the house. That's until he would start getting on my nerves. I looked at Seth and smiled. "Yes, babe, I'm so ready to go home." We both laughed.

Ms. Debra walked into the room. "Gabby, I'm so proud of you. You've come so far these past few months." Ms. Debra smiled.

I could see she was holding back tears. I reached for her hand. These past few months, for me, had been a real challenge. Ms. Debra was there to help me overcome so many obstacles, both physically and mentally.

"Thank you, Ms. Debra. Thank you so much! I couldn't have done it without you."

Ms. Debra smiled and said, "All glory goes to God, sweetie. And, give yourself some credit, too. You're the one that put in all the sweat and tears."

Clasping my hands over hers, I pulled her in for a hug. "You're the best!" I kissed her cheek.

"Go home, rest your feet. You deserve it!" she replied.

There's a tradition at the hospital, and it had to do with when a patient gets better and is able to go home, then the nurses would put up banners all over the hallway, to cheer farewell to the patient. I looked up at Seth. He was smiling harder than me, as he stood over me, ready to wheel me down the hallway. Seth unlocked the wheels and wheeled me out the room that I'd been laid up in for the past five months. As soon as we were in the hallway, all the nurses started clapping and whistling.

Tears fell from my eyes as Seth wheeled me past other patients' rooms. A few patients sat at their doors in their wheelchairs and cheered me on too.

"All this for you, babe." Seth smiled.

I took one last look over my shoulder. I escaped the nightmare of not being able to walk again. Now, I had one more nightmare to escape!

***

### Lakewood

*"This nigga house smells like straight moth balls,"* I thought to myself, as I looked through Kiles' mail.

When Hotboy told me to check up on Kiles, I didn't know how much fun it would turn out to be. I stalked his house for a full week. Every day, I waited until he went to work, hoping I'd stumble upon something in his apartment that would give me some info about him and his goings-on.

"Seth, Kiles," I said to myself, reading his mail that I'd picked up from the counter. *"So this dude's been dropping some work off,"* I thought, laughing to myself. I placed the mail back on the counter. I could have sworn Kiles was a fuck nigga. The inside of his house looked shady. The walls to the room were decorated with wallpapers portraying images of Al Capone, "Baby Face" Nelson, "Pretty Boy" Floyd, Alvin "Old Creepy" Karpis, "Machine Gun" Kelly, and some G-Men. I pondered over the quote on the Al Capone wallpaper, and it read: *I am like any other man. All I do is supply a demand.*

I texted Hotboy to let him know I was at the spot. "Oh, snap!—This nigga got the new *Madden* video game in the kid's room," I said to myself. Turning my eyes away from the game, I sighted a picture on the nightstand. I went closer and picked up the picture, looking from Kiles to the woman next to him and a little boy in the picture.

"Holy cow!" I exclaimed, my eyes widening in surprise. The woman next to Kiles in the picture was none other than Newton.

"Hotboy ain't gon' believe this!"

# Kingpen

## Chapter 3

### Eastwood

As soon as Dame dropped the shank, I ran to pick it up. Hotboy clutched his chest before falling down to one knee. I wanted to rush to his aid, but first, I had to take care of business.

"Aye!" I said to Dame.

He faced me. My fist came down right on his chin. I walked off before his body could hit the ground. I wasn't a skilled boxer like Hotboy. But once 250lbs. of pressure hits you, you'll think I was Mike Tyson.

I walked over to the other two inmates that I had put to sleep. I kicked one hard in the stomach, then his nuts. They thought they had balls to come at me and Hotboy the way they did. I was going to crush their spirits. The inmate rolled around on the nasty shower floor, holding his balls.

I walked over to the other inmate, who was still asleep, snoring. I knew I had hit him hard, but not that hard. I gripped the shank and drove it under his chin. His eyes popped open instantly. I dug deeper as the inmate reached for my hand. I went as deep as the shank would let me, killing him.

His friend watched from a distance, as he cried for his now dead homie. I walked over to him.

"Please!" he begged.

"Please!" I taunted. I was way past the tears and the pleas. I used my foot to turn him over.

He tried his best to get up. I kicked him again, this time in his face. Blood splashed on my foot. His hands went from his balls to his face.

I looked over to Hotboy. He was still on his Kapernick shit. "Who sent y'all?" I asked the inmate. He still had his hands covering his face.

"You fucked my shit up, man—I ain't gon' ever be able

to have kids," he said.

"Nigga, you ain't gon' live to see tomorrow, if you don't tell me what the fuck I want to know!" I shouted.

He looked over to his dead homie. He knew the chances were slim to none that he would make it out of this alive. Yet, he had to shoot his shot.

"Dame—he said he was gon' pay us for helping him get rid of Hotboy. We didn't know you was gon' be here. This had nothing to do with you!"

"Yeah, it did! You fuck with Hotboy, you fucked with me!" I paced with the shank in my hand. "Why Dame tryna get at my lil' homie for?" I asked.

The inmate looked at Hotboy before he spoke. "Dame—he said Hotboy's a snitch!"

I looked over at Hotboy. Hotboy looked over to a sleeping Dame. Hotboy stood up on wobbly legs and walked over to me. I knew that look. There would be no survivors today!

***

## Hotboy

Eastwood was on his best Pink Panther shit. We didn't have the time to be interrogating anyone. We were already on borrowed time. The C.O. controlling the showers would come in at any second to turn the water off.

I hunched over in pain. My adrenaline had begun to slow down. Since my adrenaline slowed down, I was able to feel the effects from my stab wounds. It felt like someone was holding a lighter to my skin with unlimited fuel. Every time I tried to move, sharp pains would shoot through my entire body.

"Nigga, you ain't gon' see tomorrow, if you don't tell me what the fuck I want to know!" Eastwood said.

I didn't see the point in trying to see who sent them to

kill me. I figured we kill them and figure the rest out later when we're safe on the wing.

The inmate looked from Eastwood to his dead homie. He was contemplating whether he should try his hand at saving his life. The only way he could do that was by going against the code—snitch!

"Dame—he said he was gon' pay us for helping him get rid of Hotboy. "We didn't know you was gon' be here. This had nothing to do with you!"

"Yeah, it did! You fuck with Hotboy, you fucked with me!"

Eastwood hesitated before he continued.

"Why Dame tryna get at my lil' homie for?"

The inmate looked at me and said, "Dame—he said Hotboy's a snitch!"

The statement caught me off guard. I could understand a nigga tryna get at me for stepping on his toes, or for fucking with his bitch. But snitching—that was something that I was allergic to. I can't even be around a snitch without breaking out.

Eastwood looked at me with a slight grin. Even he couldn't believe it. "Who he supposedly snitch on?" Eastwood asked, using his fingers as air quotes.

I stood up with shaky legs and walked over to where they stood. I wanted him to lie in my face. The inmate looked over at Dame. Dame stirred.

"He snitched on Uncle Marvin. That's how he got off on them murders and dope. He testified on Uncle Marvin." He looked at Eastwood, hoping he'd convinced him.

"On Marvin!" I spat. "Bitch ass nigga, you 'bout to die fo' som' shit you know non' about!" I grabbed the shank from Eastwood.

"Naw, homie, I got this one!" Eastwood snatched the shank back from me.

"Bitch ass nigga tried to jump me!"

The inmate tried to get up but slipped on a piece of

soap. Eastwood swung the shank, catching him in his ear. "Bitch ass nigga!" Eastwood said while stabbing him.

"Come—come on, cuz!" the inmate pleaded. Eastwood plunged the shank in his neck multiple times.

"Disrespectful bitch! I'm Eastwood Piru!"

Eastwood even had me scared. He walked over to me with the shank in his hand, blood dripped from the tip onto the shower floor. He stared at me with a menacing look.

"Clean up on aisle three." He held the shank out for me to take.

I looked over to Dame. He was still laid out on the floor. Blood leaked from his head where he hit his head on the floor. The blood, mixed with the water, made it look more pink than red.

I accepted the shank. I walked over and slapped the shit out of Dame. His eyes popped open. He was scared shitless, seeing two naked men standing over him.

"Dame, huh?" I asked. He tried to sit up. "Who put you up to this? Who put the hit on me?"

Dame looked over to his two dead homies. "Fuck you! You gon' kill me anyway! I ain't telling you shit!"

Eastwood kicked him in the face.

"You damn right you fin' to die. Matter of fact, fuck this bitch ass nigga!" Eastwood kicked him again. Dame tried to fight for his life, until I caught him in his throat with the shank. I lost my train of thought. I pictured Gabby falling over the rail, our baby dying, never seeing the world. I saw Gangsta's body hanging from a beam in the infirmary. I stabbed him until Eastwood shoved me to bring me back. When I came to, I looked around the shower. There was blood everywhere, along with three dead bodies.

"Let me see that." Eastwood reached for the shank.

I raised my arm up to hand it to him. A sharp pain shot through my side. "Fuck! That nigga got me good." I looked at my side.

Eastwood looked and said, "Damn, sho'll did. We gots

to worry 'bout that later. We got to clean this shit up, and fast." He moved fast, trying to clean off some of the blood. "Get your towel, clean as much blood as you can. We'll need to make sure yo' blood ain't on the scene." He ran off in the direction of the toilet. I heard the toilet flush, then he ran back to the shower. He dragged each body under a shower head, and turned the water on, letting the water wash the blood off of Dame, and his homies' bodies.

"Who you think sent them?" Eastwood asked.

I shook my head, clueless. "I don't know, but I'ma find out!"

# Kingpen

## Chapter 4

### Seth

"Ayee! Straydog, my guy!—What do I owe this visit?—I thought we weren't supposed to meet again, until next week," Dub said, as he blew marijuana smoke in my face.

"Your people didn't tell you? Something happened with the last pack. I was told to pull up on you to get another one."

I stepped inside. He closed the door behind me, placing the dead bolt on the lock. "Give me a sec." He placed his pistol in the small of his back.

He walked to the back room and closed the door behind him. I took a seat on the couch. My brain was going haywire. I leaned back on the couch. My arm accidently knocked a pair of jeans on the floor. I picked them up and held them up to the light. They were too small to be Dub's. I was about to lay them down, but I noticed a slit in the front, kinda like the one Kelly had in hers the last time I saw her.

Dub walked back in the room, closing the door behind him. "Okay, my guy. Everything is all wrapped up and ready to go. Do me a favor—Don't fuck this one up!"

I laid the jeans down and walked over to the bar. "Kelly—she came by my house a few days ago," I said, still thinking about her.

Dub lit a cigarette and said, "Yeah? What she say?"

"Nothing, really. She said how she'd been clean for a few months. And she wanted to see our son."

Dub blew smoke in my direction and laughed. "Why did you even get her pregnant? You knew she was a slut!"

My eyebrows rose. I didn't care what she did. She was still the mother of my son, and no one had the right to talk about her but me. "Don't—don't talk about her like that! She was a good girl when I first met her. That was, until I started doing drugs. She just wanted to get high because I was doing it."

I thought back to how I had ruined Kelly's life. She wanted to be a schoolteacher. She had a passion for kids. When she had Jacob, she was so happy. When I introduced her to meth, she couldn't stand to look at him. I sat and thought on how I had been the one to introduce Kelly to meth.

All of a sudden, a loud thump came from the back room. "Did you hear that?" I asked Dub, looking to the back room.

Dub looked over his shoulder and said: "Something probably fell." He pulled his pistol from the small of his back and laid it on the bar, putting his cigarette out in an ashtray. "I'll holla at you in a couple of days—Tell my people to handle his business better, and don't fuck that one up," he said, sliding the pack across the counter.

"Seth," a familiar voice called my name from a distance. My head turned as soon as I heard my name. I thought that I was tripping. "Did you hear that? It sounded like someone called my name."

Dub looked at me with a blank expression. "You tripping, bruh. Ain't nobody here but you and me. Let me find out you back on that dope." His eyes trailed to the ripped jeans on the couch.

My eyes followed his. His eyes went to me, then to the gun on the bar.

"Seth!" My name echoed louder this time.

I leaped for the gun as soon as I saw Dub flinch. I grabbed the gun with shaky hands, pointing it in his direction.

"Wooo, my guy! What's all this for?" He stood up with his hands in the air.

"Kelly, is that you?" I yelled, my nerves running wild.

Dub laughed. "Homie, I told you. Ain't nobody here but me and you." He stepped closer to me; his hands still raised. "Stray, bruh! Give me my gun back, and I'll think about not fucking you up."

I ignored him and walked to the back room.

"Stray! Where you going?" he shouted at my back.

I faced him so he wouldn't get any ideas. I twisted the doorknob.

"Oh shit! Kelly!" I ran to her side. I kneeled beside her and laid her head on my lap. "Kelly, can you hear me?" I laid the gun on the floor, rocking her in my arms. Dub slowly crept toward the gun. I picked it up and pointed it at him.

"Get the fuck back!" I yelled.

"Seth," Kelly whispered harshly, her voice shaky as she spoke with her eyes closed.

Tears fell from my eyes. "What did you do to her?"

"I did what she asked me to do. She came by begging that I get her high. I'm a drug dealer, it's what I do."

The gun shook in my hand, as I tried to steady my breathing. "Meth—it doesn't do you like this!" I picked Kelly's arm up; track marks with fresh blood spots caught my eye. I looked to the bed; a syringe, and a half empty cap of heroin sat beside it.

My finger had a mind of its own. I didn't want to kill him, but my finger pulled the trigger. The gunshots echoed inside the small room. The pistol was heavy, but the trigger was light. I hit him two more times before his body dropped.

Kelly opened her eyes. I looked down at her. She cringed with a smile. "Seth, you came for me."

# Kingpen

## Chapter 5

### Lt. McFee

"Wait! Do you see that?" I studied the blood-stained footprints. The footprints started at the toilet and ended at the concrete slab. I squatted down. With my gloved right hand, I touched the bloodstained print. I rubbed my pointer finger against my thumb, bringing my fingers to my nose, then I inhaled.

"It's blood," I said. "Someone almost did a good job at covering their tracks. See!" I pointed at the prints, still squatting down. "The tracks stopped at the concrete slab. So, whoever killed those three inmates, tried to clean up the blood in the shower. I'm guessing that whoever it was, walked to the toilet, flushed the murder weapon, and dressed to leave. And I can almost guarantee, without a doubt, we're dealing with more than one killer. And I have just the idea who it might be!"

\*\*\*

### Hotboy

"Hotboy, Los been looking for you. He said somebody keeps hitting his line up for you. He said to tell you, he was in the middle of something, so make it quick." Eastwood handed me the cellphone concealed inside a Bible.

I looked over my shoulder to see if Lil' Chris was awake; he was still asleep.

"Did he say who it was?" I asked, wondering.

Eastwood shook his head and said: "Naw, he ain't say. Just check in the call log, it should be in there."

I stepped closer to the bars. "Have you heard anything about the issue?" I whispered.

# Kingpen

"Supposedly, they got som' free world detectives here. Scratch told me they been here all morning. That's why they canceled showers this morning, 'cause the shower is a crime scene right now. The warden was walking around asking questions. The hit squad tore A-wing up. I guess that's the wing them niggas stayed on."

I nodded, then winced in pain. Eastwood looked at me and said, "You good, bitch?"

I nodded. "Yeah, I'm straight, shit just hurts like hell. Kuda gave me some gauze and tape. It's holding up, but I'ma need stitches."

"You gon' have to make it do what it do. For now, at least. If anyone, and I mean anyone, go down to medical, with any stab wounds, you'll be a suspect." Eastwood was right.

I was in helluva pain, but I be damned if I go down for three murders. I had to tough it out. "Yeah, you right," I said. "Fuck it, just, keep me posted. But, let me check and see who was calling for me so I can get bro' his shit back. You know how he is; he'll start crying."

Eastwood laughed and walked off. Careful not to wake Lil' Chris up, I set a sheet up to block me. I scrolled through the call log. Noticing Lakewood's number, I dialed it.

"You called?" I whispered as he answered.

"My nigga!" he said excitedly. "I was in that fool's spot today. You ain't gon' guess what I saw."

I was barely able to hear him. I turned the volume up on the phone and said, "I couldn't hear you. Say what you said again."

"I finally got inside Kiles' spot. The lawman that you sent me to"

I could hear him clearer. "Did you find anything?"

The line fell silent for a brief second. "I found Newton!"

He lost me. "I thought you said you got inside Kiles' spot. What she got to do with anything?"

He sighed. "That's what I'm saying. When I was in his spot, I saw her. She looked way different in her free-world clothes, but I'm sure it was her. When I was leaving, they were pulling up. He helped her out the car into a wheelchair."

I sat on the edge of the toilet, trying to gather my thoughts. Lakewood had to be mistaken. It had to be someone else, not Gabby!

"Hotboy, you there?"

"Yeah, I'm just confused. Are you sure it was her?"

"Unless she got a twin!"

I shook my head, wondering '*How*?' Then it all came back to me. When I first met Kiles on L-wing, he called me *Kingsley* without me even telling him my name. I couldn't understand why he was so quick to hustle with me. He didn't even know me. I recalled how Eastwood said Dame and his homies were housed on A-wing. The same wing that Kiles last worked on, when he claimed to have flushed the pack.

"*He set me up!*" I thought to myself.

"That weak ass white boy!" I yelled into the phone.

"What's up, bitch?" Lakewood asked.

Lil' Chris stirred in his sleep. I hung my head feeling like a straight *simp*. I got hit with the whooptie-blam, by a white boy, a C.O. at that!

"That nigga, Kiles. He had to have paid Dame to off me," I tried to explain.

A shadow crept up outside my cell. I took the curtain down and stood up. I could still hear Lakewood talking in the background. I laid the phone in between the mattress and the bunk. I walked to the bars and stood face to face with Lt. McFee. He looked at me, then over my shoulder, then to Lil' Chris, who was sound asleep. "Who were you talking to?" he asked.

I looked down at Lil' Chris. "Damn, bitch!" I yelled loud enough to wake him up. "I was talking to you, and you just fell asleep on me!"

Lil' Chris stared at me confused, until he saw the Lt. standing in front of the cell. "My nigga, that shit was boring as hell," Lil' Chris said, playing along.

McFee stared at us, trying to read our faces. He looked from me to Lil' Chris. "Cut the bullshit! Cut the light on! Both of you, step to the door, and show me your hands."

I walked over to the light and pulled the string, turning the light on. The bright light made Lil' Chris shield his eyes with his hands. I glanced down at my hands, hoping I didn't have any cuts or bruises on them. I walked to the door and held my hands out in front of me. McFee examined them, then he looked up to my face.

"What happened to your eye?" he asked. The blood clot was obvious that I'd been in some kind of scuffle.

"I—uhh—I was training, hitting the pads. I didn't slip the punch when the trainer told me to. Ended up getting caught in the eye. Hurt pretty bad too!" I faked a laugh.

McFee stared at me. He knew I was full of shit.

"Both of you, step to the back of the cell!" he demanded. He pulled a single key from his pocket, placed it in the keyhole, and unlocked the cell door. I took a step back, preparing myself to beat his ass like me and Uncle Marvin did the last time. Fat bastard didn't learn his lesson. I would have to grab the phone and flush it without him seeing it.

Lil' Chris grabbed his shoes and put them on.

"Get out of 'em!" he ordered us to take off our clothes.

Lil' Chris adjusted something under his nuts and said, "What's all this for?"

I took off my shorts.

"Three inmates were found dead in the shower last night. I'm just doing a routine check. Plus, Gianni, you know how you like to play with knives, don't you!" McFee smiled.

He wanted a reaction out of me. One that he wasn't

gon' get.

"Shirt, too!" McFee said, more to me than Lil' Chris.

I hesitated, looking to Lil' Chris. He looked nervous as hell. Shid, I was too. One look at my wounds, and I'll be right back on the bus to await trial for three more murders.

Lil' Chris fidgeted again. He grabbed at his shorts, like he was trying to keep something from falling.

McFee noticed. "What are you over there doing?" McFee asked Lil' Chris. "You know what, Kingsley, step back, you take off your shoes, and your shorts."

I silently thanked the game God for watching over me as I traded spots with Lil' Chris.

Lil' Chris took his time taking off his clothes. "Take off your shirt!" McFee said, agitated.

Lil' Chris chuckled lightly while taking his shirt off, tossing it to him. McFee moved his hands over the shirt, squeezing it, shaking it, hoping to find something. Coming away empty-handed, he tossed the shirt on the floor.

"Take off your shorts, too!" McFee demanded.

Lil' Chris slowly stepped out of his shorts, being very careful, as if he was hiding something. He handed the shorts to the Lieutenant.

"Boxers, too!" McFee said.

Lil' Chris looked back at me, shook his head, and laughed. I didn't know what exactly he was laughing at, but this was a serious moment. I didn't find it funny.

"Hey! I'm talking to you! Boxers, too!"

Lil' Chris looked to the ground, then to the Lt., and said: "Fuck, you!"

He caught me and the Lieutenant by surprise. "What you say?" McFee asked, shocked.

Lil' Chris took off on McFee. The Lt. had no chance of defending himself from the hard punches Lil' Chris threw his way. Lil' Chris shoved McFee to the side, and ran out the cell, screaming: "Help!"

McFee yelled into his walkie-talkie. "Flash, flash,

flash! This is Lt. McFee, I need assistance on H-wing. I have an offender on the loose, possibly carrying contraband, looking to dispose of it." He ran off behind Lil' Chris.

I didn't want Lil' Chris to get caught, but the game God had other plans. As soon as McFee took off, I ran to the phone under my mattress. "Hello!" I whispered, as my heart raced.

"What the fuck just happened?" Lakewood asked.

I peeped out the cell to see if the Lt. had doubled back. "Never mind that!" I said, still peeping my head out the cell. "I don't have much time. I need for you to stay on Kiles' tail, he's up to som'."

"I'm already on him, as we speak."

"I need you to do me another favor, too."

"Name it, and I gotcha!" Lakewood said.

"You know McFee? The fat bastard that works up here. I need you to send him a message. I'll text you the address right now."

"Overstood! I gotcha!"

"Aye! When you do it, make sure he knows it's from me!"

***

### Lakewood

I hung up the phone from talking to Hotboy and shook my head. He had too much shit goin' on.

I plugged my phone into the car charger, dropping it to the floor as I heard gunshots. "Oh, shit!" I ducked.

The shots came from inside the house that Seth went in. I had followed Seth from his house to a nice suburban neighborhood. I'd been waiting outside in the car for a minute, waiting on him to come back out.

***

Knowing police would be on the way, I contemplated pulling off. I cranked the car up just as Seth walked out the front door. He wasn't alone. He carried a woman in his arms, trying his best not to drop her. He finally got her safely in the car, looked around, making sure no one saw him. He closed the passenger door and went around to the driver's side.

It was a good thing he couldn't see past my tent. I watched him pull off, shaking my head. "What the fuck, Hotboy! What you then got caught up in!"

"*Woof, woof, woof!*" a dog barked as I jumped over a tall fence. "This nigga better be lucky I got love for him!" I said to myself. "Got me jumping fences, breaking into people's houses and shit!"

I walked to the patio door of the country-style house. I peeped through a window, hoping no one was home. I pulled my .380 ACP out and took a deep breath. I looked through the window. Two small dogs barked at me, like vicious pit-bulls. I walked to the side of the house to a window that had an A/C unit screwed into it. I looked around first, tucked my .380 in my waistband, and began to remove the unit.

I finally got a screw loose enough to snatch the unit down. The curtains blew in and out the window. I stepped on top of the unit. Sticking my head through the window, the dogs barked like an alarm system. I looked around. I could hear the shower running, so someone was home. I climbed through the window, stumbling over a footstool. I pulled my .380 back out as the dogs barked loudly. I ignored their cries and walked over to the bathroom. The door was slightly ajar. The two dogs ran under the bed and barked from a safe place.

"Max! Cat! Be quiet, will ya's!" a lady yelled from the bathroom.

# Kingpen

I pointed my .380 at the bathroom door, praying whoever it was didn't come out. I didn't want to have to kill anyone. And I damn sure didn't want to go back to prison, especially for murder. I just came to relay a message.

I peeped in the restroom, by looking through the glass mirror. The shower curtain was closed. I could make out a woman's body by her shadow outline. She was on the heavy side. But she looked like she had a fat ass.

I eased the door closed. Turning around, I bumped into a nightstand, knocking a picture to the floor. I picked the picture up and looked at it. I couldn't believe I was actually in Lt. McFee's house. I always hated the fat pig.

Beside his picture were two plaques that he received from the military, along with a military knife. I picked the knife up and held it up to the light. His initials where engraved on it: S. McFee. I looked at the knife, then to the two dogs under the bed. They both held their tongues out as saliva dripped to the floor.

"Come here, Max, Cat," I whispered. I held my hand out for them to sniff. They both eased from under the bed, as I pulled a piece of beef jerky from my pocket. I opened it, and held it out to them. They both jumped to get a piece as I snatched the jerky higher. I broke the beef jerky in half and held the two pieces over their heads, forcing them to sit. They both sat down, wagging their tails, tongues hanging. I tossed both pieces on the floor. They pounced on it so fast. Their small jaws struggled to chew the tough meat. Seizing the opportunity, I stepped on both of their tails, making them whimper and cry out. Drawing the military knife, I drove it into the skull of the smaller one, killing it instantly. The military knife was so sharp, that it went straight through the skull.

The other dog, seeing his playmate bleeding, gnawed at my shoe, trying its best to get free. I pulled the knife from the dead dog's skull. I balled my fist up and punched the other dog in the nose. The cry that came out almost sounded human like. I reared my hand back with the knife in my hand and came down hard on the dog's neck.

The water from the shower stopped. "Babe, is that you?" the lady asked.

I dug into my back pocket, pulling out a newspaper article, and tossed it on the floor. I hurried to the dresser and grabbed a red lipstick and wrote on the mirror that was attached to the dresser.

*'Let the dead bury the dead! G.K.'*

# Kingpen

## Chapter 6

### Hotboy

"Shit's crazy, ain't it!" Eastwood said, as we looked at the Echo newspaper article.

"Four bodies found dead in six months, on the Beto unit. Two inmates were found dead in the shower this past Tuesday. The motive was presumed to be gang related. There are no leads, and no witnesses. If you have any details—" I read out loud. I shook my head at the article. 'The Echo' was run by inmates from another unit. They actually had the nerve to put, 'If you have any details—'

Snitching was on public display. The game was fucked up.

I handed the article to Eastwood.

"Two bodies, only, two! —The way we hit them niggas up, it was overkill—Shouldn't nobody had survived," Eastwood said, looking back at the article.

"We got to find out which one survived, and where he's at. As on now, he ain't snitched, or we would be locked up."

"How you figure he ain't snitched?" Eastwood asked. I could hear the worry in his voice.

"Because we still moving around. Trust me, if he snitch, you'll know!"

We walked down the hallway. Eastwood walked in front of me. "There go yo' girl." He pointed at Grain as she walked in the chapel.

I looked around Eastwood and smiled. I hadn't seen her since the last day she worked on H-wing. That night, we talked about practically everything. How she hated working here, but did it to get a step closer to becoming a cop. How she had to work overtime a lot to take care of her twins. Twins! Looking at her, she didn't look like she ever had a kid, yet she had twins.

"I'll catch up with you later. Let me see what's up with

her." We locked up before he walked off.

I knocked on the chapel door, catching her attention. She looked up from what she was looking at and smiled. She was sitting in a computer chair behind a small desk. I pointed to the door, indicating that I wanted her to let me in. She couldn't hide her smile as she walked over to the door.

She unlocked the door and stuck her head out. "Can I help you?" she smiled.

"Come on, ma. Stop playing and let me in."

She looked at me, then to the watch on her wrist. "You have to leave when E-wing comes in. You know them Bible thumpers be snitching." She stepped to the side to let me in.

"Leave them people alone. All of them ain't no snitches, I got a couple of homies that's over there that just want to change their lives."

She locked the door behind me and put her hands on her hips. "Whatever! So, what have you been up to since the last time we saw each other? Probably been busy gettin' on somebody's nerves." She laughed.

"If you asking if I've been giving another female som' play, then the answer is no. Actually, I've been thinking 'bout yo' short ass." I teased.

She laughed and shoved me in my side. "Ahhh!" I winced in pain. I raised my shirt up. Blood started to seep out of the wounds that I had covered with gauze and tape. Seeing the blood spread through the gauze, Grain's eyes sprouted in her head.

"Gianni! What happened? You need to go to the infirmary." She panicked, grabbed her walkie-talkie, and brought it to her lips.

I placed my hand over hers and stopped her. "No! I'm good, ma. I just need to clean myself up. Open the restroom for me, and let me clean the blood up."

She stared at me, contemplating calling for medical assistance. Hesitantly, she put the walkie-talkie down.

"That's a lot of blood, Gianni."

I placed my hand over the gauze and applied pressure. "I'm good, I swear. Just lock the door, and let me clean myself up. Five minutes, that's all I need."

She looked at all the blood on my hand and said. "I'm scared, that's a lot of blood."

I laughed. "Ma, trust me, I'm straight. I've been through way worse. Now, are you gon' help me, or are you gon' let me stand here until I bleed to death?"

She gave me a half smile. "One second," she said, then ran behind the desk to grab something. She ran to the door with a piece of paper, placing it on the glass of the door, facing outward.

"What was that?" I asked.

"Restroom sign," she answered, as she led the way to the officer's restroom. She unlocked the door and turned the light on. I looked around the restroom for the first time. It was weird seeing a toilet without a sink attached to it. The mirror that mounted the wall above the sink was real glass. Unlike the ones in the cells.

I stepped inside the restroom and removed my shirt. I saw the lust in her eyes, as she stared at my chest. I leaned my back against the sink to get a better look at the bleeding wound through the mirror. Grain reached her hand out and touched the wound. I flinched at the feel of her soft hands, making her draw her hand back. I sensed her uneasiness.

"Grab those paper towels over there for me, get a few," I instructed, pointing to a paper towel holder on the wall.

She grabbed a handful. I raised my arm to give her room to wipe the blood off. "How did this happen?" she asked.

"Oh, uhm. I did it at work, in the sign shop."

She stopped, looked up at me, and said: "You wouldn't lie to me, would you?" She continued to dab around the wound carefully.

"Only to protect you."

# Kingpen

She stepped between my legs, reached around me, and wiped the blood that had tracked down my side. As she tended to my wounds, I couldn't help but stare. She wasn't the baddest bitch in the world, but she had helluva sex appeal. Her build, for me, was perfect. She was only four foot ten. She looked light as a feather She had long black hair, with blonde streaks. She kept her hair pulled back in a tight ponytail. Her hair looked wet, like she had just got out of the shower. I had visions of pulling her ponytail, while smacking her on the ass. Her skin looked smooth. Her skin was the color of vanilla. She had big, beautiful brown eyes. When she blinks at me, I lose my train of thought. Her lips, oh my, damn, her lips! They stayed glossy. They looked juicy and soft.

Grain looked up, catching me in a daze. "Why are you staring at me like that?" she asked.

I licked my lips like LL Cool J, and said: "Because you're sexy as hell."

She blushed. "Look at us." She gestured to us with her hand. "If we get caught, I'm gon' lose my job, and they'll ship you."

"You sound worried."

She tossed the bloody napkins in the trash. She looked up at me with those beautiful eyes, and smiled. "Never worried, always cautious."

She stood between my legs. Even though she had finished the task, she still didn't move. Standing on tiptoe, she leaned into me, eyes closed, as our lips met for the first time.

Her lips were just as I expected. Juicy and soft. I was always a kisser that kept my eyes open. I'm glad that I did, seeing that she had closed hers. As our lips danced, I eased off the sink. I turned her to where her back was now against the sink. I sucked on her bottom lip. Her left hand touched my cheek. A soft moan escaped her lips as her right hand found its way to my dick.

40

I trailed kisses down her neck. Her hand traced the outline of my dick. I started biting and sucking on her neck, leaving a purple passion mark. She reached into my boxers, her fingers touching the pre-cum from the tip of my dick. She gripped my shaft, moving her hand up and down, bringing me to my full length.

Our tongues connected again, as they played their own symphony. I had to place my hand over hers to stop her. She was just stroking away.

"Hol' up, babe!" I said. It felt damn good to feel her small, soft hand squeezing my dick, but I wanted to feel something else. She looked up at me, embarrassed. I reached for her pants and unbuttoned them. I stared into her eyes as I unzipped her pants, never breaking eye contact. I turned her, making her face the mirror. She pulled her shirt above her ass, making her pants fall to the ground. She had the sexiest ass I've ever seen. Her red Victoria's Secret panties were cut perfectly with her cheeks. I kneeled behind her and closed my eyes. Her scent was mind- blowing. She smelled as if she'd just sprayed a bottle of Chanel perfume all over.

I spread her cheeks, her sex lips waved hello. Easing her panties down, her vagina sat perfectly between her legs. I was the one that was bleeding, but I made up my mind: I was about to hurt her pussy.

I separated her sex lips with the tip of my tongue. Her back arched, forcing her to lean over the sink. "Ohh, my gawd!" she moaned.

I stuck my tongue deeper inside her tunnel. She reached her hand back, and gripped my head, forcing my tongue deeper. My face was buried inside her ass cheeks. "Oh shit! Uhmmm—oh my god! Father—please forgive me!" she moaned as she threw her pussy back on my tongue.

I was a skilled pussy eater. I felt that I had to be, as much as I talked the talk, I had to be able to back it up. The way she was twerking on my tongue let me know I was doing my job.

"God can't save you, ma!" I stood up, picked her up, and eased my way inside her tight box. Her walls closed around my dick. She was so tight I thought I was in the wrong hole. Every time her ass bounced off my balls, she panted, and said a different word.

"Oh—my—gawddd—fuck!" she moaned.

I was so caught up in seeing myself in the mirror, fucking a C.O., I forgot where I was. I bit down on my bottom lip to add to my porn star facial expression. I was making my own porno.

I gripped her ponytail and turned her head to the mirror, so she could see exactly what I was looking at. Her facial expression was so sexy. She moaned, looking at herself, then bit her lip. I was digging in her pussy like I was trying to bury my dick there forever.

I felt myself on the verge of climaxing. I wasn't ready to bust yet, so I slowed down my pace. I substituted fast pumps for slow, steady pumps. I wanted her to feel like she was on a roller coaster ride. I hit the bottom of her pussy with one hard thrust after another.

"Gianni—Kingsley! Fuck—meeee! Fuck me, harder!" she begged.

I pulled out, picked her up, and placed her on the sink. She fitted perfectly as I brought her to the very edge. I leaned forward and kissed her. My dick found its way back home. "Damn, bae, you got a pretty pussy," I complimented her tight, juicy box.

I fucked her with one hard thrust after another. Her hand went up to my chest, as I placed my finger on her clit. My finger became her clit's personal trainer. I refused to let a bitch say she didn't cum when I fucked her.

"That's it, bae! Right there—fuck!" she managed to say.

I fought with everything in me not to bust. Every time I came close, I would slow down my pace. I had niggas trying to kill me, so just in case this was my last shot of pussy, I was gon' enjoy it.

"Cum with me, babe! I want to feel it inside me! Shi—iit, it feels soo good!"

She watched my dick slide in and out of her. She placed her hand around the base of my dick, gripping it every time I came out. That shit turned me on to the max. I picked up my pace again.

"Ohh shit! Yes-ss—fuck me like that, babe!" she screamed.

My dick was covered with her cream. Every time my dick went in and came back out, her cum would slide down to her pretty pink asshole. That shit was so beautiful I couldn't control myself. I gripped her titties through her uniform shirt and exploded inside her.

"Argghh!" My body jerked, as my seed fought to get a taste of her sweet pussy. I was so spent that I couldn't move. We both stayed in the same position for a brief second, both of us breathing heavy, our bodies glistening with sweat.

Then she smiled and said, "Again!"

# Kingpen

## Chapter 7

### Newton

"Jacob! Get the door for me, babe!" I yelled from the bathroom. I wheeled myself to the living room to see who was ringing the doorbell.

Jacob took his time. The doorbell turned into hard knocks. As Jacob unlocked the door, Seth rushed in carrying a woman. Her face was buried in his chest.

"Seth, what happened?" I asked, seeing the blood on his pants.

Seth ignored me? "Jacob, move those pillows out the way," he said.

Jacob moved in a hurry, hearing the command from his father. Jacob grabbed the pillows, tossing them to the floor. He tried to look and see who the woman was. Seth gently laid the woman down on the couch. She reached out to Seth. Her hand caressed his face. I wheeled myself closer to see who in the hell was caressing my man's face.

"Seth! No, what the fuck is going on?" I asked, seeing Kelly's face. "I know you didn't bring—this bitch in my house!" I ranted.

Seth took off his shirt, tossing it to the floor. "Jacob, go to your room, and close your door," he said, ignoring me again.

Jacob looked at the woman on the couch, then back to his father. "Go!" Seth pointed and yelled.

"Seth, you're not going to answer me? I sighed. "What is she doing, here, in my house?"

"Our house, Gabby, ours—And, she's doin' exactly what it looks like she's doing, she's resting," he said, nonchalant.

"Seth, if I could stand up right now, I swear! —" I was heated. "Is that all you're going to say? And, whose blood is on your clothes?" I questioned.

He looked down at his clothes and snickered. He took a seat by Kelly's feet, and pulled out a package wrapped in black tape. He placed the package on the table and unwrapped it.

The silent treatment he was giving me was silently killing me. "Seth, please talk to me. What's goin' on?"

He scooted to the edge of the couch and pulled a gun from his lower back. He laid the gun on the table and looked at me. "I killed a man today—I shot him three times," he said, like he killed someone every day. He pulled out a green leafy substance, and one that I've grown to know so well.

Seth killing someone took me by surprise. He had never been a violent, aggressive type. I never thought in a million years that Seth would actually kill someone. "What do you mean, you killed someone?" He was starting to scare me. "Seth, you're talking crazy right now. And, what does killing someone have to do with her being in our house?"

Seth raised his pointer finger to his lips, shushing me. He looked down to Kelly to make sure I didn't wake her. I was beyond heated now. First, he comes into our home with another woman in his arms. A woman that I've always hated. Then he has the nerve to say he murdered someone, and he won't even fill me in on the details. And now, now he had the nerve to shush me in my own damn house!

"Don't you shush me! The nerve of you, to shush me—in my own damn house! For this bitch!" I spat. "The same bitch that left you and Jacob to fend for yourselves."

As loud as I was, I knew the bitch wasn't asleep. She was probably high, and Seth confirmed my suspicion as he sprinkled a pinch of meth on his finger, bringing it to his nose; he made the dope disappear like magic.

"Seth, I can't believe you're doing that shit in front of me!" He knew how I felt about people using drugs, especially him. "That bitch has got your head all fucked up. I'm leaving!" I reached for my phone that was inside my fanny pack.

Seth stood up fast and mugged me with a look that I had never seen from him before. He walked up to me and said. "You're leaving! Why? So you can run off and be with your precious Gianni!" He caught me off guard. "Huh?" he continued. "Have another baby with him, like you did the first time!" he yelled.

"Seth, what, what are—"

He cut me off. "Shut up, bitch! What, you think I'm stupid? You thought I didn't know, huh? Thought I was just som' dumb ass meth head! You thought that you and him could just pretend that y'all didn't happen. Well, guess what, Gabby! I saw the text! I was the one that took your phone! I saw the fucking sonogram! I even saw the sonogram under your pillow at the hospital!" He picked the gun up from off the table and pointed it at me. "You still love him, don't you?"

Tears fell from my eyes, my hands shook uncontrollably. "Seth, please babe. Put the gun down."

He shook his head with his eyes closed. "Answer me!" he yelled.

I closed my eyes. This had to be a dream. This had to be the vision that I saw in the hospital.

Seth walked up to me, grabbed my chin, and placed the barrel of the gun to my temple. "Answer, me!" he said through clenched teeth.

Tears fell freely as I squeezed my eyes shut. I was too afraid to open them. "No!" I said with my eyes still closed. "I don't love him! I love you, Seth. I made a mistake! Can we just—please—talk? Just put the gun down."

"A mistake, huh? Yea, me too! I made a mistake when I left Kelly for you! See, all this time, I blamed Kelly for leaving me and Jacob. But it was really my fault. See, Gabby, I was the one that introduced her to this!" He piled some more meth on his fingertips. "See, if it wasn't for me, she wouldn't be in this predicament." He sniffed the dope from off his finger. "I started messing around with you while I was still with Kelly. You convinced me to get clean. And when I did, I thought I was too good for Kelly."

As he talked, his nose started running. He leaned over the table to take another hit, this time from the whole package. He took a whiff, leaned his head back, and sighed while letting the dope drain. Meanwhile, he kept his gun pointed at me. "See, Gabby. Now, I have my family back. Jacob can finally meet his real mom, and Kelly, can finally be a part of Jacob's life. The only thing that's standing between us, is you!"

"Seth—please!" I sobbed.

"Oh, don't worry. I know how much you loved you som' Gianni. So, I'm gon' send you to him!" He grabbed the handles on my wheelchair. Swinging the chair around, he shoved the chair to the kitchen.

"Seth, stop! You don't have to do this!" I yelled.

He stopped, like he had just thought of something. "I didn't tell you, did I? Your baby daddy's dead." He stood in front of me, his gun at his side. "While you were laying up in the hospital, crying over a bastard baby, I was working my ass off on the Beto unit. See, at first, I wanted to make him suffer for taking you away from me. That was until I saw the baby picture under your pillow. You never really loved me, you used me. I was your little experiment. I know how you like to 'fix' people." He grilled me and finished. "So, tell your baby daddy, and your baby, I said, burn—in—hell!"

Seth walked around me and opened the basement door. He grabbed my wheelchair, determined to flip it over on top of me. I held on to the door handle for dear life.

"No, Seth, I'm sorry! Please—Seth!" I begged.

"Save your tears, you've cried enough for Gianni Jr." He shoved me, then kicked me.

"Somebody—help me! Please!" I screamed, praying someone could hear me.

Jacob ran in in the kitchen. He stared at his father as he slapped me around.

"Daddy, stop! You're hurting her!"

"Jacob, shut up and go to your room!" Seth yelled.

"Jacob, baby, go to your room, please!" I said to Jacob. I wasn't sure what Seth had planned for me. Whatever it was, I didn't want Jacob to witness it.

"Bitch, let go!" Seth punched me as I held on to the door handle. He didn't care that Jacob stood there watching. I prayed to God that Jacob wouldn't grow up thinking hitting a woman was okay.

Seth punched me again, pulled me by my legs, forcing my grip loose. I became dizzy, my vision blurry as he rained blow after blow at me. "Seth, please!" I begged as blood leaked from my mouth.

My cries fell on deaf ears. Seth punched me one last time; my mind was a blur. I visioned the day when we first met: *Seth and Jacob watched as the ice cream truck passed by them. We were in a park in Dallas. Jacob was so little then. Seth was doing his best to take care of a kid by himself. I remember walking up to him, speaking to Jacob. He looked up at me and smiled. He was so cute. Seth told him, "Say hi, Jacob." Seth's voice gave me chills, like my soul had been dying to hear his voice. Jacob looked at me and grinned. "Hi," he said innocently. I thought he was so adorable. "Hi, Jacob, my name is Gabriela." I held out an ice cream cone that I had bought from the ice cream truck. His eyes lit up as he looked up to his father for permission. Seth nodded, and Jacob snatched the ice cream cone like he hadn't ate in days. That was the last time I saw them, until three months later, by chance; I was introduced to him at a get-together, at a friend's party. Seth had cleaned up good, but he had lost a little weight. We talked the entire night, me mostly asking about him, his son, and Jacob's mother. That night, I felt an instant connection to Seth. I gave him my number, and a week later he called from pre-*

*paid phone. We met up for lunch; well, we ate hotdogs from a hotdog stand. That's where we shared our first kiss. That was the day I fell in love with Seth Kiles.*

What I couldn't understand was, who was this man in front of me now that held a gun, pointing it directly at me. Seth let off a single shot, the echo sounded louder than it should've. I couldn't feel the impact, but I knew I'd been shot. Blood began to cover my shirt under my right breast.

Seth grabbed my legs and threw them over my head; the rest of my body followed as I tumbled down the basement stairs. Jacob stood at a distance and screamed. "Mommy!"

Through all the pain, I still managed to smile. Jacob still called me his mommy!

## Chapter 8

### Lt. McFee

"Come in!" the Office Inspector General answered from behind his office door.

I turned the knob and walked in his spacious office. I was semi jealous. I've been working in Texas corrections for over ten years, and I still have to share an office with multiple people. I've busted over fifteen inmates with cell phones, twenty inmates with narcotics, and twenty-five C.O's trying to bring drugs to inmates. So, I can say, I've earned my own office.

"Sean, how can I help you?" O.I.G Thompson asked, calling me by my first name.

"We have a problem, sir," I said, placing my hands behind my back. He looked up from his laptop and said, "What's the problem?"

I gestured to the empty seat. "Can I?" He nodded. "Kingsley," I said, taking a seat. "The inmate that went to trial a few months back on the murders of C.O. Bryant and an inmate. I think he's at it again."

"So, you're saying that Kingsley's the one connected to the bodies that were found in the shower?"

"No! I mean, yes. Well, I'm assuming, sir. See." I pulled out a newspaper article. I handed it to him. "This was left at my house. Along with *this*". I showed him a picture of my wife's two dead dogs.

"*Let the dead bury the dead. G.K,*" Thompson read out loud.

"G K, Gianni, Kingsley!" I said.

"But how? He's in here?" he asked.

I shrugged and said, "I'm not sure. I'm guessing he had some outside help."

"So, you're saying, an inmate. One that we both know killed a fellow officer and an inmate, yet he got away with

51

it. And, he's killed two more inmates, and may get away with that too." He then smiled.

I looked at him like he was crazy. "Did I miss something? What's so funny about this?" I asked.

Thompson leaned forward in his chair. "This is perfect!" He stood up, excited "Do you remember when I first started?"

I nodded. "Yes. I was a sergeant then," I recalled.

Thompson smiled. "I was new on the unit. The first black Office Inspector General in this region." "No one liked me. But you, you kept me busy. You found ten cell phones in a month. And when you brought them to me, what did I tell you?"

"You told me that if I kept up the good work, you would make sure I became a lieutenant."

"Did I come through for you, or not?" he grinned.

"Yes, you did." I looked at the bars on my collar.

"I need you to do one more thing for me, and I will make sure you get what you've been working so hard for."

I looked at him with wide eyes. "Are you serious, sir?"

"Sean, it's time. I talked to my boss, and he's giving me a promotion. Well, I have to earn it. One more big bust, and the job is mine. And when I become the director for this region, who do you think I'm going to leave my job to?"

I smiled and looked around the spacious office. I had worked my ass off from day one of working here. I started off as a C.O., because of my military background. After a year, I put in to become a sergeant. I met Thompson when I became a sergeant. He was new on the unit, and unwanted. No one wanted a black Office Inspector General on an all-white unit. Majority of the staff, at that time, were dirty officers. The Aryan Brotherhood ran the unit. Anything they wanted, they got. Majority of the staffing officers being ex-KKK members, easily followed suit behind the Aryan Brotherhood. For weeks, the staff were paid to trash Thompson's office. Some even did it for free. One day, his car is egged and spray-painted with racial slurs. The next, his house gets a brick through the front window. Instead of quitting, like everyone thought he would, he came to work early every day. And made sure to be the last one on shift to leave. Within a month, the entire staff of dirty officers were fired and indicted for organized crime. At that time, I was caught up in trying to be a good law, and trying to stir the dirty C.O's that I knew away from the bad side. Thompson promised me that if I helped him get rid of the dirty laws, he would make sure I became a lieutenant. Seeing the bars on my shirt, he was a man of his word.

"What is it that you need me to do, sir?" Whatever he wanted, I was all in.

Thompson stood up, walked around his desk, and sat on top of it. "My whole career has been to make the world a safer place for our families, by keeping the bad guys where they belong. When we first started, we were unstoppable. We busted a different dirty C.O. every other week. But now, they're getting smarter, and they're working together against us. The only way that we can keep up with the new age crooks, is to think like them, move like them, and hope that they'll slip up, so that we can catch them." He pulled out a small bottle of liquid from his pocket. "This, Sean, is the treat, to catch the trick."

"What is it, sir?" I asked curiously.

He tossed a small bottle to me and walked back to his chair. "It's the key to this office. That's, if you really want it. See, Sean, that's pure, potent K2 spray. Bought it straight from the black market. That, there, is going to turn the unit upside down, and it's going to get us both a raise, and multiple convictions."

I stared at the bottle. It looked like water. It was the size of an eye drop bottle; only it had a spray nozzle on it. I looked at the label, it read: 'Not for human consumption'. The actual ingredients were in a language that I couldn't comprehend. "How is this the key?" I asked.

"We're—no! *You* are going to spread that across the unit. Start an uprising, if you have to. We have to make the unit look like it's out of control, so we can swoop down, and save the day."

I looked at my mentor of five years in complete shock. For years, we took down the bad guys. Now, the man that I looked up to, wanted me to stoop down to a criminal's level. I got inmates' time stacked on their sentence, for spreading poison on the unit. Now he wanted me to join them. This was the unit that I laid my life down on the line for. The unit that I sacrificed my time and marriage for. And for what? A promotion! "Sir, I don't understand! We're against this." I shook the spray bottle for emphasis. "Why would you want me to spread this?" I asked.

He stood up and walked to his wall of certifications. "Sean, you see this wall. Every accomplishment I received was from doing the right thing. For getting convictions for inmates, and for C.O.'s that thought they could come into the system and outsmart us! When Kingsley got away, he showed us that we were slacking. He showed us that we can be outsmarted. I had no explanation why one of our female officers was stabbed to death in an inmate's cell. The state lost sixty thousand dollars taking Kingsley to trial. Just to find out—he didn't do it!" he yelled.

"Sir, we both know he did it. I also feel that he's the one behind the two bodies that were found in the shower."

"That may be true. But in order to take him to trial, we'll need more evidence. Solid, concrete evidence. Something that he can't pin on another inmate."

"I have a footprint, a bloodstained print that I found in the shower."

"Not good enough! We had the murder weapon, and the dope from his cell. That wasn't even good enough! We have to get him this time."

"How do you propose we do that?"

"With that! We set him free. We give him just enough

rope to hang himself. I have just enough evidence to prove that Kingsley was, in fact, at the scene of the shower the day of the murders. The camera shows him leaving off the wing with his shower materials, but it's not enough for a conviction. If we were to bring Kingsley's name to the DA, they'll probably laugh in our faces."

Thompson reached for the bottle; I handed it to him. "Our friend, Mr. Kingsley, he's a young hustler. He will never pass up an opportunity to own the unit."

"Opportunity?" I asked.

"You're going to give him free range, to sell as much of this as he wants. In exchange, we get half the profit and in a nick of time, he'll have this entire unit dying from an overdose. When the warden finally comes to grips that the unit is out of control, we'll come in and save the day."

"Sir, but what if Kingsley turns us in?" I was worried this wouldn't play out like he wanted it to. He didn't know Kingsley like he thought he did.

"Oh, I'm sure he won't. Kingsley's one of the last of a very rare dying breed. He'll never snitch, no matter what the circumstances are—"

"Kingsley's not going to trust me when I come to him with this. He's a convict, not an inmate. He will see me, then go the other way."

"Sean, trust me! Bring him to me and let me do the rest."

I shook my head. I prayed in the end of all of this, that we would come out on top. Knowing Kingsley, we probably would end up as another notch under his body count.

# Kingpen

# Chapter 9

## Hotboy

"You heard what happened?" Eastwood asked me as we sat in front of the TV.

I shook my head and said: "Naw, what happened?"

"The chaplain called Los to the chapel. Supposedly, somebody killed his cousin."

I looked from the TV to Eastwood. "Dub?" I asked.

Eastwood nodded and said, "Yea, they say somebody killed him in his spot. Hit him up a few times too."

I hung my head. "Damn, that's fucked up!"

"Yea, I know! It seems like every time we get shit going good for us, everything crumbles all at once." Eastwood managed to laugh it off.

I was lost in thought. He was right. Every time we got shit going for us, some bullshit would happen. As I was in my own world, Bullet—a big Caucasian—walked over to the TV and changed the channel. Bullet was a huge nigga, standing at 6'7, 230lbs, all muscle. Bullet lifted weights every day. "I'm sorry, y'all—My ma told me to watch the news—She said something 'bout som' coronavirus crap that's killing a lot of people," Bullet explained as he surfed the channels.

Eastwood leaned forward on the bench. He was on the verge of standing up, until I grabbed his arm and shook my head. I knew what was running through his mind. He felt disrespected by Bullet changing the channel. We had way too many problems to be worrying about fighting over the one-eyed devil.

Bullet pointed to the TV and said. "See, breaking news!"

"The coronavirus, also known as COVID-19, is a breaking force. COVID-19 has spread across the globe faster than any virus in history. First discovered in China, the COVID-19 virus has broken records in death tolls, ranging close to three hundred thousand, nationwide. Masks are becoming compulsory. Governor Gregg Abbott has issued a mandatory curfew, starting tonight at 11:59. For more—" the news reporter finished.

Everyone in the dayroom looked around at each other. We all had our own theory going on in our minds. "Aww, shit! They don' made God mad now! He fin' to kill all the sinners!" Eastwood joked.

A few of us laughed, some of us took what he said seriously.

"Well, y'all better have y'all lockers full, 'cause sooner or later, they gon' lock this bitch down, watch!" Bullet added.

As we listened to Bullet talk, two C.O's walked up to the window from the outside. "Damn, they scared the shit out of me!" Eastwood said upon seeing them.

The two C.O.'s raised a metal frame the size of the window and bolted the frame over the window. Bullet tapped the window with his knuckles and said, "Aye, what's up? What's that for?" he asked the C.O.'s.

They both ignored his question, moving along to the next window. Everyone in the dayroom fell silent, our minds thinking the exact same thing. "Hell naw, them hoe's tryna cage us in this bitch!" Eastwood shouted.

The two C.O.'s went from one window to another, adding extra protection to every window. I figured, like everyone else did, that they were adding extra protection to keep us from escaping. But why? Why all of a sudden would we want to escape? Both of the dayroom TV's turned red, with a loud blaring emergency system sound. The noise startled me, as I jumped damn near in Eastwood's lap.

"Scary bitch!" Eastwood shoved me.

The news reporter from CNN News walked up to the podium, with a fearful look in her eyes. She cleared her throat before speaking. "The president has issued a state of emergency!"

***

**Newton**

My head was throbbing so bad my neck was sore, but not broken. Thank God! I felt like someone was holding a fifty-pound weight to my chest. All I could remember was, me and Seth arguing, and then we tussled, then he shot me. I can't believe he actually shot me. The whole time I was unconscious, I thought this was all a dream. Seeing that I was lying on our basement floor, it wasn't a dream. It was my reality.

I tried to move my legs, but they wouldn't budge. My body felt like I'd been shoved over three row all over again. I winced in pain as I tried to crawl. I raised my shirt; seeing the small blood-covered hole in my chest made me cry.

I looked around for anything that I could use as a crutch. With only the light from a small window, I was able to make out a small couch, and the washer and dryer.

"Ahhhh!" I yelled in pain as I tried to crawl to the couch. I lifted my waist band to see my hip bone sticking straight out of my hip. The pain was excruciating. I lifted my head as tears fell down my cheeks. "Why me, God?" I questioned the most high, hoping for a reply.

When I didn't get one back, I figured he was too busy to be dealing with a saint's request. I couldn't tell how long I'd been unconscious. Seeing the blood on my shirt and pants was still wet, I figured it couldn't have been too long. I had to get some help, and fast. I wasn't a doctor, but I could tell by looking at my hip, I was in bad shape. I felt woozy. So either I hit my head pretty hard, or I lost a lot of blood. Then it came to me. "My phone!"

I felt around the floor for my fanny pack. The basement door opened. The bright light from the kitchen forced me to cover my eyes with my hands. I guess I'd been down here longer than I thought. Seth pulled the string to the basement light, taking the stairs two at a time. I looked at his face and could instantly tell all he's been doing was, get high. His facial hair had started to grow in, making him look older than his age. "You're awake, good!" Seth said, "That means I won't have to drag you." He held a heavy chain in his right hand. My life had made a drastic change overnight. One day, me and Seth were madly in love. The next, he's trying to kill me. It was like he was a totally different person.

I looked at the dangling chain and got chill bumps. Just the thought of what he had planned for me had me seconds from peeing my pants. "Seth, can we talk? Please! Look, let me go, and— and I swear, I won't tell the police."

He sucked his teeth and said, "Yea, right! I admitted to killing your boyfriend. And I admitted to another murder. After what I did to you, you expect me to believe that! I'm high, but I ain't stupid!

"He walked up to me, the metal chain scratched the floor. The sound sent chills down my spine. "Seth, wait! I swear, I could never take you away from Jacob! Think about Jacob! He loves me, Seth, please! Please, don't do this to me."

"I can't kill you, but since you can't walk, you're going to stay down here until you bleed out." He killed what little hope I had left.

Me and my big mouth. He's going to let me die down here, by myself. He's using my pain for his own advantage. At least he wouldn't kill me, like I thought he was about to do. Waiting till I bleed out could take days, hopefully.

"I hate that you drove me to this point, Gabby," Seth said, as he walked up the stairs. He dragged the heavy chain behind him. As he made it to the top of the stairs, I noticed my fanny pack under the stairs. Seth took one last look at me before he turned the light off, closing the door behind him. As the darkness took over the basement, I kept a mental picture of where my fanny pack was. I thought about how I was going to get it. My phone was my only chance at surviving. I was getting weaker by the day, and getting to the phone would be painful, but I would rather die trying, than to die laying it down.

# Kingpen

## Chapter 10

### Hotboy

"This shit crazy, homie. They locking the whole state down for this weak ass corona virus shit!" Eastwood said as we watched the news.

"Dumbass nigga!—The whole world on lockdown, not just Texas—Yo' fat ass know how to make some money, but you ain't got no common sense," Sirpreme joked.

Sirpreme had recently got shipped to Beto from the Ferguson unit. Sirpreme being from Dallas, got moved to Beto, to be closer to home. Sirpreme was my new celly. He was older than me, but so far, we got along good.

"Fuck you, nigga. They said state of emergency, not worldwide emergency." Eastwood tried to plead his case, as we all laughed at him. I looked at Eastwood and shook my head while pointing to the corner under the TV. We had a ritual on Beto, wherein if you do, or say anything stupid, you have to stand under the TV while you face the wall. Most people refused and wouldn't go. That's when our security team comes in. They'll wrestle you down, pick you up; whatever they had to do, just to get you under the TV, they'll do it. Eastwood could've bucked, big as he is, but he went willingly. As he excused himself to go to the corner, I stared at the window. I was still stuck on them putting the metal frames over the windows. That shit just didn't sit right with me.

"What's up, bitch? You alright?" Eastwood asked, as he sat back down.

"That shit there." I pointed to the window. "That shit fucking with me. Something ain't right, homie. I'm telling you."

"Nigga, you goin' hard! —Stop overthinking shit— They probably put that shit on there to keep the bugs out," Eastwood said.

"Homie, this unit been up since the 90's. They sho'll waited a long ass time to want to keep the bugs out. What they really tryna do is, keep the animals in."

"How you figure?"

"They already had bug screens on the windows. What the fuck they need that other shit for? Now they talking about som' coronavirus bullshit that's killing people. Think, my nigga!"

Eastwood nodded and said, "Makes sense. But—shi'd, we alright—for now. When they start doing som' off the wall shit, then we panic."

"One row! Rack time!" the C.O. working the wing yelled to the dayroom.

I looked over to Eastwood. "Can we panic now?"

"Why you think they racking us up?" Sirpreme asked, as we made it to our cell. He took his shirt off, exposing his hairy chest. He tossed his shirt on his bunk. I never understood why niggas rocked the hairy chest look. He was on som' straight caveman shit.

"Don't get me to lying," I said as we stood beside each other, looking down at the other rows. Niggas was running around like it was the end of the world. Scrambling to get food, books, and other shit from their homeboys. Every time we got racked up randomly, for whatever reason, it was always the same. A nigga would be a damn fool to go straight in his cell without anything to eat or read.

There was no telling when we would be able to come back out. Beto was known for hitting us with the whooptie-blam. They'll tell us to rack up for special count, and we wouldn't come back out for another thirty days.

"Hotboy, y'all good up there?" Eastwood yelled from one row.

"I'm straight—I just need some legs—I need to get that issue from the spot, then I'm good!" I shouted.

"If they don't put the porters up, I'll come to you with it. If they do rack us up, then I'll pull up when they do showers in the morning."

"That's a bet, 'preciate ya," I said, then walked in the cell. I laid on my bunk. I was mentally exhausted. Ever since Los's cousin got killed, we've been trying to survive off of the little dope we had left. I had yet to contact Kiles since Lakewood discovered that he was somehow related to Gabby. I was still tryna figure out how I was gon' play that whole situation. For some reason, I felt that Kiles was the one behind the shower hit. I wasn't a hundred percent sure, but my instincts told me that he was, and I always trusted my instincts.

"I'm tired of this shit!" Sirpreme said, as he sat on top of the sink. He placed his foot on the toilet seat and said, "They slowing a nigga money down." I placed both of my hands behind my head. I didn't know how much longer I could take this shit. I was due to see parole any day. It couldn't come any faster.

# Kingpen

## Chapter 11

### Seth

"Hey, Kiles! Where have you been? I haven't seen you in a while," Sanderfield said as I walked from the warden's office.

I got my ass chewed out by the warden because I missed three days without calling in sick. I wasn't planning on coming back to work, until Kelly convinced me to. She told me that it would look suspicious, considering that Gabby was missing, and I had stopped going to work. I had to make everything look normal.

I was just happy that Kelly didn't flip out on me once she found out that I had beat and shot Gabby. Kelly was actually happy that I finally decided to let her come back in Jacob's life. Jacob was the one who was hurting the most from all of this. Since the fight, he's been crying non-stop, asking why I hit Gabby the way I did, and why I shot her. I was so high when everything went down, and I didn't know Jacob was still standing there when I shot her. So, I lied to him. I told him that the gun was fake, and that me and Gabby was just playing. I told him that she's staying at her mother's house for a few days. Being that Gabby's been the only mom he's ever known, it's hard for him to understand when I tell him that Kelly's his real mom. He's young though, so he'll get over it one day. I walked to F-wing's picket; I received the keys from the key boss, who was impatiently waiting on me to relieve him of his post. After letting myself in the picket, I locked it back.

Sanderfield watched me from outside the picket, with her hands on her hips.

"What's up?" I asked, catching her watching me.

She sighed and said, "Nothing, I'm just saying I was talking to you, and you just completely ignored me.

I honestly had forgot that she said anything to me. I was

so caught up in my own thoughts that I wasn't really paying any attention to her. "Damn, pretty. My bad! I just got a lot going on, is all. What were you saying?"

As soon as I called her *pretty*, her attitude went out the window. Sanderfield was one of those young chicks that craved attention. If she didn't get it, she'll catch an attitude. But when you gave her some attention, she was beyond gullible. "I was just wondering where you've been lately? I haven't seen you in a few days, just making sure you're okay," she said, as if she really gave a damn. She was just nosey as hell.

"I know. Shit's been fucked up lately. I haven't been able to sleep. Gabriela hasn't come or called in a few days. I'm worried about her." I put on a sad face. I figured I might as well start my alibi with Sanderfield. Knowing how loose her lips were, by tomorrow, everyone would know what's going on.

"Are you serious? Are you talking about the girl that's on your Facebook page? The one that used to work here?" I nodded. "That's so sad, why though? Did y'all get into a fight or something?" she asked.

"No!" I said, nipping that scenario in the bud. "We didn't get into a fight. She just said that she needed some space. I respected her wish, but now, it's been a few days, and I haven't heard from her. Not a call, text, nothing! It's taking a toll on me." I looked away, like I was trying hide the fake tears that were falling. I had to make it seem real as possible.

"I'm so sorry, Kiles. I can't imagine what you're going through. You know, you should file a missing person's report. A few days without hearing from her, that's not good."

The picket phone began to ring.

Excusing myself, I picked up the phone. "E, F, G, H-picket," I spoke into the phone.

"This is the infirmary—I need an offender from H-wing. Cell three-thirty-four, inmate Gianni Kingsley. He needs to come down to the infirmary for his yearly shot."

Hearing Kingsley's name caught me by surprise. She had to have had the wrong name. I was sure that Gianni was dead. I paid to get him off'd. They found the body in the shower. She must've had the wrong name, or some old records.

"Hellooo! Can anyone hear me?" the lady yelled on the other end.

"Sorry, yes! I heard you, but did you say, Gianni Kingsley? Are you sure that you have the right name?"

The lady sighed, like I was irritating her. "Yes! I'm sure! I'm looking at the roster; he's in three- thirty-four. I need him down here asap, please!" The lady hung up.

I held the phone in my hand. Before I got out the car to come to work, I had hit a nice size line of meth, so I was high, but not that high to realize that Gianni's not dead.

"Kiles, are you alright?" Sanderfield asked, sensing my change of mood.

I hung the phone up and said, "Yes, umm—I'm good. I just still can't get Gabriela off my mind. Can I ask you something?" She nodded. "Has there been, anything—like—crazy happened since I've been away?"

"Crazy, like what?" she asked.

"Like, people getting hurt," I said.

She thought for a second. "Ohh, you talking about McFee's house? How someone stabbed his dogs?" She went over my head with that. "Or are you talking about the bodies that were found in the shower?"

When Sanderfield said *bodies*, I knew the lady on the phone had to have made a mistake. I leaned on the picket gate, placing my arms through the bars. I said: "What!" I played surprised. "They found a body in the shower? When? Who was it?" I bombarded her with questions.

"No, not body, but bodies. It was two guys from A-wing. Dame and this guy that used to always be with him."

# Kingpen

My heart felt like it had fell to the pit of my stomach. I was sure Gianni was dead. This whole time, he's been alive, and he killed the inmate that I had paid to kill him. He was more dangerous than I thought. I wondered if Gianni knew that I was the one behind the attack. And if he did, what was his next move? Would he come after me next? My mind was all over the place.

"How did they die?" I asked.

"Someone stabbed them multiple times. It was horrible. I was able to see the bodies as they were wheeled out on gurneys, right before they zipped the body bags up. They had the shower taped off. I swear, it looked like a scene straight from a movie. I had never seen anything like it before."

She drifted back to the scene in her mind. I couldn't help but wonder what Dame told Gianni before he was killed.

"Sanderfield!" I snapped her back to reality. "Can you do me a favor? Tell H-wing's boss that three-thirty-four is needed in the infirmary right now."

I had to see Gianni for myself. I had to be sure that he wasn't one of the ones that they found in the shower. I silently prayed that he was one of the ones they found. I know praying death on someone wasn't right, but God just had to understand, you can't love everybody.

"What's the inmate's name?" she asked.

"Gianni. Gianni Kingsley!"

## Chapter 12

### Hotboy

"Kingsley!" the wing boss yelled, waking me up out of a deep sleep. "They need you in the infirmary, right now, C.I.D."

I was having a dream that I had made parole, and I was able to walk out of the front gate of the unit. Grain picked me up in a candy apple red corvette. She was looking good as hell, too. Babe even got some ass shots to add to her exotic look. I stretched, with a slight yawn. I rolled over, looking to the clock on the desk. The time read 11:10. I must've dozed off, waiting on Eastwood to pull up with the issue. Seeing that he never brought it, they must've racked him up too.

I yawned again, raising my hands above my head. I looked at the cell door, noticing that it was already open. I stood up and looked at a sleeping Sirpreme. He was lying on the top bunk, asleep, with his headphones on.

I walked to the sink, wondering why they were calling me to the infirmary for C.I.D.

C.I.D was for yearly TB shots that they made us take, to prevent us from getting sick. I wasn't due to get mine for another six months.

After I brushed my teeth, and washed my face, I stepped out the cell, locking the door behind me. I didn't want anyone trying to sneak into the cell while I was gone. It was bad enough that I didn't hear the door when it popped open.

Sirpreme was asleep with his headphones on, so if anyone was to sneak in, he wouldn't even hear them.

I walked down the stairs. The wing looked and sounded deserted. All I could hear was faint sounds from radios, and light snores. Eleven o'clock was considered early in prison. But once you went in the cell, within thirty minutes, you were going to sleep. It was something about being in a small area, with limited things to do. It always made me go to sleep, even when I wasn't sleepy.

"H-wing out!" I yelled as I walked up to the gate.

Sanderfield walked up to the gate, holding a set of keys. She hid a smile behind a mean mug. "Where you tryna go?" she asked, just to start a conversation. I wasn't up for her bullshit tonight. I was fresh out of my sleep, from a badass dream. All I wanted to do was, go to the infirmary and come back, so that I can go back to sleep, in hopes of finishing that dream.

"My nigga, stop playing with me! Y'all just rolled my door to go to the infirmary," I said, agitated.

She placed a key in the keyhole, then looked up at me and said, "Let me see your ID." She was trying to get under my skin.

I huffed, and pulled out my ID. I held it out at a distance, not letting her touch it. She turned the key to let me off the wing. I stepped off the wing. She eyed me as she closed the gate behind me. I walked down the hallway in a hurry. The quicker I can get to the infirmary, the quicker I can get back to my bunk.

As I made it to the infirmary, I turned the doorknob. I held on to the door for dear life as the wind tried to snatch the door from my grip. I had to fight hard to get the door closed. As I got the door closed, I looked to the cage, where the inmates sat, until our names were called. The cage was completely empty. Not a single person sat in the cage. I looked around, wondering what the fuck was going on.

As soon as I saw who was working the infirmary, I knew what the deal was. Grain swayed up to me with a medical mask covering her mouth and nose. A lot of C.O.'s had started wearing them for safety precautions. She pulled the mask down, exposing her juicy lips, and smiled. Her hair was pulled back in a tight ponytail, just like I liked it. She placed her finger to her lips and grabbed my hand.

"Grain, what the hell, ma. What you got goin' on?" I asked, as she led me up a set of stairs that led to the second floor of the infirmary. She faced me once we made it to the top of the stairs.

"Stop calling me Grain, call me Stephanie—We're past that officer, inmate crap," she said, opening the door.

I followed behind her with caution. I had only been to this section of the unit, twice. Both times were when I first got to the unit.

"Don't worry, everyone is already gone—Nobody is up here," she said. She unlocked the GI's office door and stepped inside. I hesitated as I looked over my shoulder. As sexy as she was, I wasn't trying to get caught up. Most niggas that got caught up, got caught right before it was time for them to go home. Seventy-five percent of the time, they got took down by fucking with a bird brain, careless bitch. Beto had a curse that I wasn't trying to keep alive.

"What about the nurses downstairs?" I asked. "Anybody can come and walk up on us." This was the first time in my life that I was actually scared to get some pussy. I was so nervous I knew my nigga wouldn't perform the way he usually do.

"Babe, calm down. Majority of the nurses went home. They're scared of that coronavirus crap. They're only allowing two nurses on shift at a time, just in case one gets sick, she won't get everyone sick. There's one in the ER, and one in the back." She rubbed my cheek with the tip of her finger. "Trust me, babe, mama got you." She smiled.

She pulled my shirt, practically dragging me in the office. She closed the door behind me, locking it. Her lil' short ass was feisty and bold.

"Ma, you wild. You went through all of this for me?" She stood on tiptoe and wrapped her arms around my neck.

"I haven't been able to stop thinking about you, Gianni. I don't know if it was the dick, or how you make me feel altogether. All I know is, I can't get you out of my head."

She stared into my eyes.

Our lips met. Her eyes glowed beautifully through the computer screen light. I connected with her, too. I just couldn't let her know. I had fell in love with Gabby the same way. I put my trust in what I thought we had, and she stepped all over it. Gabby ruined my emotional connection for every bitch to come.

"I can't lie, ma, you cool peoples," I said.

Her lips curled as she shoved me. "Really, Gianni! That's it? Cool peoples! I actually thought you liked me." She turned her back to me and walked to the GI's desk.

I sighed and ran my hand through my waves. It was like every woman that I met in the penitentiary fell for me. I knew I was a helluva catch, but damn!

"Come on, ma. What you want me to say? I mean, I care about you, but we just met. You're beautiful, independent, smart, and you're about that life. But in order for there to be more, you would have to show me you're worthy."

"I know we just met, but you could've said something other than 'cool peoples'. You make me feel like what we did was nothing. Like I was just som' quick release for you."

I shook my head. I couldn't, and never would be able to, understand women. They were more complicated than a Rubik's Cube. "Grai—I mean, Stephanie. It ain't even like that. You know I cut for you, ma. I just got a lot on my plate at the moment." I pulled her to me.

Her back laid on my chest, her ass instantly brought heat to my midsection. My nigga woke up, stretched, and nudged her cheeks,

"Gianni, I know you're in prison, so yea, you keep your guard up. But I'm not the enemy. I'll ride for you." She fought for my heart.

I kissed her behind her ear, tracing my tongue along her neck. She relaxed, unfolding her arms, and let out a soft moan. "You talking like you ready to break a nigga out this bitch, or som'." I laughed as I continued to kiss her soft spots.

"Mmmmmhh, I will, if you want me to. Ughhh, stop! You not gon' keep doing me like, this!" She panted.

I kept sliding my tongue over her ear lobe. I was driving her crazy. I couldn't believe she said she would break me out of here. I knew she was just blowing smoke. She was bold, but she wasn't that bold.

"Gianni, stop, bae! That's my spot!"

I gripped the inside of her thighs. They were so soft. I gripped the soft flesh, right beside her pussy. "That's yo' spot, huh? Let me see for myself," I said, as I unzipped her pants.

They fell to the floor. I reached over her to the computer mouse. I moved the mouse, making the light to the screen come back on. This time, I wanted to take my time with her. I didn't want to miss anything. I started unbuttoning her shirt, until she stopped me. "Wait! I uh—I have to leave my shirt on. Just in case someone comes. That way, it won't take me forever to get dressed."

I laughed. "I thought you said we didn't have anything to worry about. So, why are you tripping?"

She stared at me shyly, her pants at her ankles. She stood in front of me with her work shirt still on. "I mean—we don't have anything to worry about. I just—"

I thumped her hand away. "If we don't have anything to worry about, then let me do me," I said, as I unbuttoned her shirt down to the last button. As her shirt fell from her shoulders, she folded her arms, covering her titties. Her purple laced Victoria's Secret boy shorts matched her purple laced bra.

Her ponytail hung down to her shoulders. She looked beyond beautiful. I couldn't help but stare at her fat pussy lips. As small as she was, you'll think she had a little pussy. Her pussy was full, and it ate her panties up like it was starving.

"Move your arm, ma—Let me see you," I said.

She shook her head; her ponytail swung from side to side. "No! Can I put my shirt back on?"

I grabbed her hands; she lightly put up a fight. "Stop, Gianni!" She pouted.

"Why?" I asked.

"'Cause—you're not going to like them." She put her head down, embarrassed. She covered her chest with her arms again. I looked at her titties through her Victoria's Secret bra. They weren't big, like most I've saw. But they were titties, and I was a man. A man in prison at that.

I walked closer to her. She stepped back, bumping into the GI's desk. "How about you let me be the judge of that, huh?" I kissed her neck.

She let out a moan that stirred something up deep on the inside of me. "Ahh—bae, your lips. They're so soft." She panted. She gradually unfolded her arms, letting her hands fall to her side. I unhooked her bra and tossed it to the floor. Taking a step back, I admired her beauty. She tried to cover herself again, until I stopped her.

"Unh uh! Put your arms down, ma. You look beautiful, can't you see?"

She looked down at herself. She twisted her foot shyly. "You're just saying that because you're about to fuck."

I laughed and said, "You damn right I'm about to fuck. I'm about to fuck you so good, the nurse is going to have to come and check your blood pressure." I kissed her lips. One hand fell down to her nipple, and the other gripped her ass. I scooped her up by her soft cheeks, pulling her up till she was standing on tiptoe.

Our kiss was so strong that we fell on the desk. I slid the keyboard over, as I kissed my way down to her titties. I sucked on her left nipple and pinched the right one. She arched her back, gripping my head.

"They're—perfect!" I said,

"Ahhh—bae! Bite it—please."

She didn't have to ask twice. I lightly bit her nipple, while pulling the other one. Her mouth opened, but no words came out. Her scent hung in the air. She smelled so good. I tried to take it slow, but her scent was driving me insane. I lightly bit her nipple, then her stomach, all the way down to her panties. I took a deep breath, inhaling her scent. She smelled like kiwis and strawberries.

She leaned off the desk, anticipating me to take her panties off. I did what her body demanded. The first time we fucked, I was able to look at her sex lips. This time, as she laid back on the desk, I was able to admire them. Just seeing her sex lips coated with her juices made my dick throb in my pants.

"Get on your knees, babe. Here." I handed her panties to her. "Put them in your mouth," I said.

She eased on her knees and grabbed her panties. "I won't be loud—I won't need these—uhh!" she said, as I stuck my tongue deep in her tunnel. "Ahh—fuck!" she screamed, as I spread her cheeks, giving my tongue more room to work. She rocked back and forth, like it was my dick inside of her instead of my tongue. "Nigga! what the—fuck—you didn't warn a bitch or nothing."

I ignored her cries as I flicked my tongue up and down her slit. I sucked on her sex lips, like a juicy mango. Her legs started shaking, "Ahh, bae—fuck!" she yelled as I stood up.

I snatched her panties from her and stuffed them in her mouth. I pulled my pants down, and lined my magic stick up with her gasping hole. I took my time easing the head in. She looked over her shoulders, her eyes screaming how good it felt. Just to make sure I was hitting it right, I pulled out. She growled at me like a dog in heat. I gripped her ponytail, wrapping it around my hand.

"This is what you woke me up out of my sleep for, huh?" I dove in her pussy like a swimming pool.

"Mhmm—mhmm!" was all you could hear as her panties muffled her screams. I squeezed her luscious cheeks as she threw that ass back like she was auditioning for a Pit Bull video. My eyes closed on their own as I fought back the urge to catch my nut.

"Damn, gurl! Fuck! This shit—explosive, ma!"

She nodded, and her head fell forward in bliss.

I licked my thumb and centered the tip at her crinkled hole. That bitch was sexy, clean, and pink, with no traces of hair. Like she had her shit waxed and bleached.

She spat her panties out her mouth and said, "Babe, you better—not!"

I stuck my thumb in her asshole. She bucked like a wild horse. "Babe—eee—fuck me! Fuck me, daddee!"

I plunged my thumb in all the way down to the knuckle. "Arhhh, babe—it feels, *so* good!" she moaned. I picked up my pace, as I gripped her hips, turning them bright red.

"You love this dick, don't you!" I pulled her ponytail tighter.

"Uhmm—yes! Fuck this pussy, babe! I love it! Fuckkk!" She threw that ass back like a pro. Her ass fit perfectly with my midsection. Every time she rocked back into me, she fitted me like a glove.

"Fuck me, babe—shit!" she cried.

I should've pulled out, but I couldn't. Every time I thought about pulling out, I didn't. Her walls would snatch me back in, like a suction cup.

"Daddy—I'm cumming!" she screamed.

"Arghh, shit—me too!" I roared as I smacked her hard on the ass. She liked that shit. I could tell how she bucked into me harder and harder. Her lil' ass was going into overdrive. I couldn't keep up; I shot my seeds in her. My body jerked as I emptied my sack. She continued to rock slowly, until my dick was too sensitive to take it anymore. I jerked two more times, then pulled out. My body was covered in sweat.

"Damn, ma, you's a fool!" I said, as I looked around for something to clean myself up with. She looked at me as she laid on top of the GI's desk. I laughed as I watched her play with her pussy. She made a nigga feel like I wasn't in prison. "Come on, ma, get dressed. I have to get back before count time. You have to get back to your post, or did you forget?"

She continued to play with herself with two fingers. Her pussy was so wet with our cum. "Sssshhh, bae! Fuck this job, fuck this prison! I just want you."

I walked over to her, leaned my head down, and softly kissed her on the lips. She opened her mouth and sucked on my bottom lip like a vacuum cleaner.

"Look, babe! Look how you make me feel." She showed me her cum-coated fingers.

I brought them to my mouth, licking them clean. "Damn, babe! You taste so good."

She laid back and spread her legs as wide as they could go. "Can you fuck my mouth, while you see how good I really taste?" she said.

My magic stick jumped. I swear that nigga got a mind of his own. I licked my lips. I knew there was a chance we could get caught, but I couldn't help myself. She tasted so sweet, and I had a sweet tooth!

# Kingpen

# Chapter 13

### Seth

I checked my watch for the tenth time as I looked down the hallway. Gianni's been gone for over thirty minutes. C.I.D normally doesn't take that long; normally five minutes, tops. The night was already too quiet, more quiet than usual. The entire unit was racked up, per the warden's orders. Most of the C.O.'s were either ducked off in the restrooms, or asleep in the closets. Sanderfield had taken off somewhere. I had to handle the picket and be the key boss. There was no way that I could dodge Gianni now. I had to let him on the wing. That was if he ever came back.

I sat on top of an aluminum trash can, waiting for him to come back. I badly needed a pick-me-up. I had a little dub sack of meth that I snuck in through my ID holder that they never seemed to check. I thought about going in the picket, up to three row, to toot my nose. That was, until Gianni walked down the hallway with a big ass grin on his face. I saw him before he saw me. As soon as he noticed me, his smile faded, he replaced his smile with a mean mug. I didn't know exactly what he knew, but by his face expression, I could tell he knew something, and whatever it was, it wasn't good.

"What's up, my nigga. Where you been?" Gianni asked as he walked up to me.

I looked up and down the hallway, hoping any C.O. was looking from afar. There wasn't a soul in sight, only us. "I—uh—I've been on sick leave. I haven't been feeling well."

He tried to read through my bullshit. I did my best to look sick. As bad as I was sweating, I knew I looked somewhat sick.

"So, what's up? You still owe a drop. How we gon' settle it?" he asked.

"I don't know, I tried calling Dub, but he never picks up his phone anymore." I pretended not to know Dub was dead. I figured I could kill two birds with one stone. I had already solidified my alibi with Gabby's disappearance. Now, I had to play the fool to Dub's murder.

"Dub ain't gon' ever answer his phone again," he said while looking at his shoes.

"What you mean? Is he locked up or something?"

He shook his head and sighed. I guess gangsters did have a heart.

"He's dead. Somebody ran in his spot, and smoked him, then took all his dope," he said. Then he laughed. "The police found over a hundred bands in the wall behind the fridge. I'm guessing it had to be a dope fiend who killed him, 'cause a real jack boy would've tortured him until he came off of everything."

I wanted to throw up. I was in so much of a hurry that night, and only grabbed the package that Dub had ready for me, along with some heroin that I had found on the floor.

"Damn, that's messed up. The few times I met him, he was cool. I really hate that for him, and of course, Los too. How's he taking it?"

"Los, he's good. Just taking it day by day."

"That's good! So, what, how are we going to produce without some work? I mean, I could just bring some tobacco, if that's cool with you?"

"Naw, I got somebody else who got some work—I'ma hit him up, then I'ma give him yo' number, then y'all can figure out the rest," he said with a yawn. He looked exhausted. If I wasn't mistaken, he smelled like sex.

"That's cool. Yea, whatever, I got you." I walked to H-wing's gate to let him on the wing. I wanted to ask him about the bodies that were found in the shower, but I didn't want to draw his suspicion. At the moment, I was in the clear. He showed no signs of knowing that I was the one that set him up.

"You be safe," he said. "I'll let my people know what's up, so stay ready." He walked on the wing.

"You, too! I heard people was around here getting stabbed and shit since I've been gone. So you be safe, too." Once the words left my mouth, I regretted them. Me and my big mouth!

As I closed the gate, Gianni looked at me and stared, never breaking eye contact.

\*\*\*

### Hotboy

Kiles' words caught me off guard. I rubbed the scar from my stab wound. The wound still hurt like hell. Every time I touched it; it took me back to the day it all happened. I stared at Kiles. I couldn't help not to. I couldn't help but wonder: *Did he know that I was the one who laid them niggas down in the shower? Or could he see the pain when I walked?* His face looked uneasy. Like he knew something. His forehead glistened with traces of sweat. He couldn't even look me in the eyes. He kept glancing at his feet.

"Yea, I heard about it," I said. "I only got the Inmate.com version of it." I tried to read his body language. *Inmate.com* was another way of saying inmate rumors. "What did you hear?" I asked.

Kiles took a step back from the gate and said, "Uhh, I just heard that two inmates got stabbed to death in the shower, that's it."

"Did they say who did it?" I asked. "Or if they have any idea of who could've done it?" As I spoke, I let my arms hang out the gate. He eyed me nervously. If he was to say my name, I was going to snatch him up through the bars and choke him the fuck out. Where we were standing, the cameras couldn't see us, and the C.O. who was working the wing was asleep in the officers' closet.

"I—uh—I don't know. I mean, they didn't say they knew. They just said that they're looking. To me, I think whoever did it will get away with it scot-free."

He cleaned that shit up real quick. He looked like he was ready to shit his pants. Whatever he knew, he played it off like he didn't know nothing. If he didn't know I killed Dame, he damn sure suspected me. I could tell by how nervous he was. "Oh well! Fuck them niggas! Niggas die every day in the penitentiary. It's a part of life. Death don't stop 'cause you're in the pen'; it's just silenced. You know how many niggas got killed by a pig ass C.O. for some bullshit? Or how many niggas hung themselves, 'cause they didn't get a fair trial. Them the niggas I feel for! Not them niggas that got killed in the shower, they could've been some fuck niggas for all I know. The way they died, it had to be God's plan."

He fidgeted and wiped the sweat that ran from his forehead to his nose. Just as he was about to say something, Sanderfield walked up. "It's count time!" she said. "So get to your cell." Her hair was all over her head. Like a nigga had just got done pulling it. She probably just got one, blessing another C.O. in the parking lot. Most likely a ranking officer. They all did it. It helped the new female C.O.'s feel special, so that they wouldn't have to work on the bad side of the unit. The ranking officer was probably some fat, knock-kneed pig, who liked fucking females his granddaughter's age. They thought that shit was live. To me, that shit was lower than the dirt that's under the sand at the beach. They all bled the same to me. A badge didn't make them more of a man than me. And their stripes that they wore on their collars couldn't compare to the stripes I earned in the streets. When an inmate wins a female C.O., the male officers always hate on us. They wonder why a woman would mess with a nigga in the pen', seeing that we don't have anything materialistic. Me, when they win, I don't get in my feelings. It's all a part of the game. Either the females gon' ride for the laws, or they gon' ride for the convicts, and get the fantasy she's always dreamed of. It's always the ones that want to be good, was always taught to be good, and prefers to be a good girl. They'll fall in love with another male C.O., hoping he'll marry her. Eventually, he'll leave her for another female C.O., and the ex will come to the dark side. She'll feel unwanted, and vulnerable. A vulnerable woman is an easy woman.

I looked at Sanderfield, and laughed. It was only a matter of time before she switched over. She'll end up doing it and won't even notice it. She just haven't ran across the right nigga. If I wasn't against using my own kind, I would've been and put my foot on her neck. 'Cause all she's looking for is a stomp down nigga.

I looked at Kiles and said, "I'll holla at you later." He nodded. I took off up the stairs to Los's cell. I walked up on him, scaring him by mistake. He had a Bible in his hand that he hurried and closed. I could see the bright light from his cell phone that he had laid down inside of a thick cut out section of the Bible. If I was anyone else, he would've got away with it. I knew better. He wasn't a Christian, he was a Muslim.

"Blood, you scared the fuck out of me. What's good?" he asked. He walked to the bars with the Bible in his hand. He peeped over his shoulder to make sure his celly was still asleep.

"My bad," I said. "I was coming to let you know, I just bumped into Kiles."

Los's eyebrows rose. We both had counted him out as never coming back to work. "What he talkin' 'bout? He do know he still owe us a drop, don't he?"

"He knows. That's what we were talking about. He's ready, he just waiting on us to get the product, then he'll take care of the rest."

"That's what's up. What else he talkin' 'bout?"

"That's really it. I had to dip off. That big nose bitch—

Sanderfield—walked up when I was talking to him. You know I try to stay out of her way."

I couldn't tell Los exactly what me and Kiles were really talking about. Los was one of the homies, a good friend too. But when it came down to the murder game, there was no such thing as keeping a secret, because a real killer never tells anyone. Running my mouth gives him power over me. Therefore, I had to take what I knew to the grave. I'll die before I ever give myself up.

"I got another cousin that be fucking around," Los said. "His shit ain't as potent as Dub's was, but shid, it's better than nothing. The way the game is right now, with this virus shit floating around, dope on the unit is at its all-time lowest. If we don't jump a point, it's gon' be a recession."

His celly stirred in his sleep. I placed my finger to my lips, reminding him to keep his voice low. Niggas would pretend to be asleep, but be really low-key eavesdropping, plotting on you. "It's good, I got a lil' homie out there that knows where to get some pills and shit—We'll use his connect, until we can come up with something better, "I said, as I looked over his shoulder, making sure his celly wasn't listening. "I need a favor—I need to use the Jaguar—I need to go to the world real fast," I said, referring to his cell phone.

He sighed, then looked to the Bible in his hand. "I was just in traffic, bitch. You lucky I love you." After a pause, he continued. "Here!" he said, handing me the Bible. "I need it back before shift change, so that I can put it up in the spot," he added.

I tucked the Bible under my arm as we shook up. "'Preciate ya, bitch. I'll bring it back before shift change." I looked at Los's clock on his stand. I only had ten minutes until shift change. I took off to my cell, keeping my head straight, being careful not to look into anyone's cell. This time of night was cutty time. All the booty bandits were capping their night off. I didn't want to be a witness to any forbidden action.

I slid my cell door open, then I slid it back to where it looked like it was actually closed. I hated being in the cell with the jag, and the door's locked. I felt like I had a better chance of escaping with the jag if they were to ever run down on me again. Locking the door this way only gave me one option, and that was, flushing it if push comes to shove. As big as this phone is, I'll be caught before I can break it down enough to go down the toilet.

Sirpreme was still asleep. The fool stuck his hands in his pants and scratched his balls, then he brought his hand to his face and scratched his nose. I laughed and shook my head. The shit people do when they're asleep, or when they think no one's watching. I grabbed my bed sheet, and hung it up from the bunk to a hook on the wall to protect myself from anyone that walked by looking inside the cell. I grabbed a fresh roll of toilet tissue and sat in on the desk. I laid the phone flat on top of the tissue. For some odd reason, the signal picked up better that way. I put the code in, unlocking the phone. The battery symbol popped up on the screen, indicating that the battery was almost dead. I had to hurry up and handle my business, because I was running out of time. They always counted before shift change.

I dialed Lakewood's number. "Ayee, what's up!" he answered, high as hell.

"Shit much, what you got goin'?" I asked.

"Shit, really. Blowing a blunt of loud, you can't hear it?" he laughed. "I'm about to get knuckles deep inside a bowl of cinnamon toast crunch in a minute."

I shook my head, laughing at him. I knew Lakewood like he was my own son. That was from doing all those years in the pen' together. Some shit he did, he just couldn't hide. "So what's up? Can you get me a half a pound of that shit you smoking on? I need to get my hands on some work, so that I can give it to my mule, Kiles. The other shit that I got is damn near gone. I'm trying to load up, just in case they lock the unit down." I peeped over the sheet to make sure no one was coming. I should've woke Sirpreme up to watch out for me. The reason why I didn't was because I knew he would want to make a call, too. And I only had like six minutes until shift change.

Lakewood smacked on his food, then burped. "I gotcha, big bro—Yo' boy sitting pretty good right now," Lakewood said.

I looked at the screen. I must've dialed the wrong number. Lakewood had his own work. Hell had to froze over. "Oh yea, you doing it like that? What can you put together for me?" I figured he was sitting on a few ounces, if anything.

"Don't trip. I'ma put som' together for you. It's on me. I owe you for looking out for me for all those years. When you touch down, I'ma lay a few stacks in ya' hand."

The phone beeped again. The battery symbol flashed across the screen. I was racing against the clock. The battery could die any second. "Get it ready for me. You know how to wrap it, I'ma text you Kiles' number. Y'all link up, I need it asap!"

"Say no mo', I gotcha. But, I love you, I gots to go. I got a bad bitch over here that I've been dying to dig into."

I laughed. "Do your thang, don't let me stand in yo' way. I'll text you his number. I'ma get at you later."

"One!" Lakewood said, hanging up.

I sat there looking at the screen as the battery symbol continued to blink. I knew I was playing with fire. But I had one more thing that I wanted to do before I took Los's jag back. "Fuck it!" I said to myself, as I logged on to my old Facebook account. Lately, for some reason, I've been thinking about my Jr. which only made me think about Gabby.

"Damn, she ain't posted anything in over a week," I said, looking at Gabby's Facebook page. I scrolled down her page until I landed on a picture of her and a little boy.

# Concrete Killa 2

She was sitting in a wheelchair, the little boy stood beside her. She still looked amazing, flaws and all. That was the last thing she posted. The phone beeped again, this time the battery symbol flashed red. Instead of hurrying up, I kept being nosey. I wanted to be sure that Lakewood actually saw what he thought he saw. I scrolled through her picture albums. I clicked on the one that read, 'Love of my life'. I was finally about to get some answer.

I clicked on the album, then the screen went black.

# Kingpen

## Chapter 14

### Lakewood

I picked up another bud of loud and placed it inside a White Owl rillo. No matter how much money I had, I always smoked out of White Owls, because White Owls were always there for me when I couldn't afford anything else. Since I was a teen, I've been smoking Reggie, corn weed, and White Owls.

I licked the White Owl, then I tucked the outside of the rillo, pearling the blunt. I've been smoking non-stop since I came up off the free bands lick. I sparked the blunt up and leaned my head back against the couch pillows. I inhaled the fruity buds as I relived the day I walked into the biggest lick I've ever had.

*"Anybody home?" I shouted, as I stepped inside. I held my Glock at my side. The way I held it, you could've mistaken me for a cop. I slowly crept through the house, following a trail of blood. The scent of blood was so strong I had to cover my nose with my free hand. The bedroom door was wide open. I raised my Glock, and aimed it in the direction of the bedroom door. I didn't want to get shot. It seemed like the closer I got to the bedroom, the more blood I saw. I squeezed my nose, trying to block back the vomit that was fighting to come up. The smell of blood always made my stomach turn. "I'm here to help!" I shouted as I stood in the doorway. As I said those words, I wanted to take them back. The nigga that was laid out on the floor needed more than help. He needed God. His eyes were still open, only lifeless. They looked like they were about to pop out of their sockets.*

*I shook my head. "Damn, homie—You got wet up by a white boy," I said, like he could hear me. He was probably already waiting at heaven's gate. I looked at his chain and watch. He had to be caked up. He had that dope boy look.*

# Kingpen

*Since I was already here, I figured I might as well see what I could come up on. As bad as I wanted to take his chain and Rolex, I had to let him make it. I knew, from experience, Rolexes had serial numbers.*

*Me, being a jack boy, I went to every spot that I knew a true hustler would most likely hide his product. I looked under the mattress, nothing. I grabbed a pair of socks that I found on the floor and slipped them over my hands. I didn't want my fingerprints on anything in the house that I touched. 'I knew my time was limited, so I ran to his closet, tossing shoe box after shoe box, until I got to an orange, Nike shoe box. I shook the box like a kid on Christmas morning. It felt heavy, too heavy to be just a pair of shoes. I walked over to the bed. I sat the box on the bed and lifted the cover. Seeing the contents inside, I did a quick dance. Never in my life had I ever saw so many rolls of money. I looked over at the dead man. It was like his eyes were staring at me. "I'm sorry, homie. It's better that I take it than the police. At least now, you can die with a good name. They won't be able to say it was a drug deal gone bad, 'cause I'ma take all the evidence."*

*His face was blank. I knew if he was still alive, he would've understood my concept. Either way, I was taking everything with me. His ghost would just have to haunt me later. I walked back to the closet, to make sure I didn't leave anything behind. His lifeless body slouched over. I knew something else had to be in there. Even in death, he didn't want to give it up. After checking every shoe box, I gained a light workout. I spotted a Gucci duffle bag that was tucked away in the far corner of the closet. Once I picked it up, I knew I'd hit for the whole shebang.*

*Tossing the duffle bag on the bed beside the Nike box, I rushed to unzip it. Seeing the neatly stacked bricks inside, I jumped up like Michael Jordan when he hit the game winning buzzer beater. I picked up a block of Kush and brought it to my nose. The fruity smell was potent. It smelt so good I could've bottled it up and sold it as cologne. Each time I stuck my hand inside the Gucci bag, I came up with a different drug. Once I took out the last item, I was staring at molly, a couple bells of Kush, some X.O's, meth, and a brick of cocaine. I rushed out of the place, tossed the whole stash into my trunk, and hopped inside my whip. I lost no time in driving off.*

Several minutes later, I was at my crib together with Mama Dee, smoking a blunt.

I jumped as the blunt burnt my fingertips. "Babe, are you okay?" Mama Dee asked. "Let me see it, does it hurt?" She kissed my fingers.

I had ran into Mama Dee at a Walmart in Palestine, when I went out there to tail Kiles. At first, she pretended she couldn't talk to me, being that I was an ex-offender, and she was a C.O. They had a strict policy, saying that they couldn't have a relationship with inmates, or ex-cons, for two years. Then, by coincidence, we bumped into each other again. This was after I came up off the free bands lick. She saw how fly I was; she saw dollar signs.

We ended up exchanging numbers, and two days later, I was knee deep inside that white pussy. I can't lie, she had me hooked. I had a thing for good, tight, old pussy.

Mama Dee went from kissing my finger, to sucking them. Her tongue rolled around them as she moaned. "Don't start, Mama—You know that freaky shit turns me on," I told her, as I grabbed my lighter from off the coffee table. I relit the blunt. There was nothing like getting some pussy while in the clouds. That's why I prayed that God allows us have sex in heaven, 'cause if he didn't I wasn't going to make it.

"You like it when I do this?" She fucked her mouth with my fingers. The bitch damn near had my whole hand in her mouth. That shit made my dick hard as hell. Old bitches took freaky to a whole 'nother level.

I placed the blunt between my lips and freed my dick

with my other hand. Pre-cum dripped out the head like it was drowning. She knew what to do next. I didn't have to say anything. She slid down to her knees, taking my dick in her hands. Her pale ass had turned me out. I couldn't get enough of her freaky ass. She never asked for the dick, she just took it. The whole time I was in prison, she pretended to like the Hispanics. The whole time, she was a nigger lover.

"Mmmhh, auhh!" she moaned, as she bobbed her head up and down.

"Suck it, babe!" I said, with my head leaned back on the couch. "Just like that," I said, with the blunt hanging from my lips. I enjoyed the sensational feeling of her lock jaw head game. Smoke ran from my nose as I took another pull from the blunt. I smiled. I loved me some freaky old bitches. It was something about cougars. They loved to prey on a young, boss nigga

\*\*\*

### Seth

I stormed in the house and slammed the door behind me. "He's not dead! He knows!" I yelled. I was going crazy.

Kelly looked from the TV to me. "Who? Who knows what?" she asked.

I sat beside her on the couch. I hit a line of ice that she had already laid out on a glass mirror. "Arhh!" I leaned my head back. The meth only added to my hallucinations. I hadn't slept in over a week. My body was tired, but my mind was geeked up. "Gianni! The one Gabby was cheating with. He's not dead! I had paid someone to kill him, but Gianni ended up killing him." I laughed.

Kelly took a smaller line and whiffed it down. "So, you think he knows that you're the one that sent someone to kill him? How? Did he say so?" Kelly asked.

I stood up. I had too much energy to sit down. "No, he didn't actually say so, but you could tell. The way he looked at me. I could see it written all over his face." I paced back and forth as the meth sped my heart beat up. I truly hated meth, but meth seemed to be deeply in love with me.

Kelly walked over to me. "Babe, calm down." She grabbed my face with both of her hands. "Everything is going to be okay." She kissed me on the lips and said, "You're overthinking things. Just calm down. We have way more important things to worry about. Like your ex downstairs."

"I had almost forgot about Gabby. I've been so busy getting high, I didn't think to check on her. Did you give her anything to eat?" I asked Kelly as I walked to the kitchen.

She walked behind me and gritted her teeth. "Did you forget that you have a lock on the door? And you're the only one with a key."

I dug the keys out my pocket. I found the right key and unlocked the lock on the door. I looked back and grabbed an apple from the fruit bowl on the counter. I tossed the apple from hand to hand as I walked down the stairs.

"Can I come, too?" Kelly asked.

I looked over my shoulder and said, "Hell no! Close the damn door and be quiet!"

She slammed the door.

I pulled the string, cutting the basement light on. I silently prayed that Gabby was already dead. She killed my hopes as she blinked to get her eyes back used to the bright light. Gabby sat up when she saw me. She actually looked frightened by me. I mean, she had every reason to be. I did shoot her, then I pushed her down the basement stairs. "You're not dead?" I stated the obvious.

She yawned before speaking. "Hi, to you too!" she said, as she eyed the apple in my hand. I could hear her stomach growling as I took a step closer. I sat on the couch and stared at her. I wish I would've went about this a different way. I wanted her dead, but I couldn't bring myself to do it. I looked down at her. She had her sweatpants pulled down under her thighs. Her bone was sticking out of her hip. She had tied her tank top around the flesh to stop the bleeding. I felt sorry for her. I wish I could take it all back, but I couldn't. This was real life; there was no going back in time.

"Gabby, I really hate how everything went down," I admitted.

"If you do, Seth, then let me go. I won't say anything, I swear! Just please—please let me go!" she sobbed.

I was always a sucker to her tears. As bad as I didn't want to be the reason for her demise, I had to. I had already said too much and took it too far. "I wish I could, Gabby. I really do. I just don't understand, I mean, why? Why did you have to go and cheat on me? What did he have that I didn't?"

She tried to sit up in a more comfortable position. She gasped from the pain from the slight movement. "I was emotionally detached from you, Seth. You had left me and Jacob for days, without reaching out to us. Gianni was a good listener. I didn't mean for it to go that far. I swear." Her tears slowly slid down her cheeks.

Anger rose on my face like a disgusting pimple. When she spoke of him, of them together, I couldn't take it. "How many times?" I asked.

"How many times, what?" she countered.

I sighed. "How many times did y'all have sex?"

She looked like she wanted to lie.

"And don't lie! For all you've put me through, you could at least tell me the truth!"

She looked down and sighed. "Twice," she said.

"Twice, huh? But I thought you said you didn't mean for it to go that far. Seems to me, the first time was so good you had to go back for a second one. Huh!" I stood up.

"Who was better?" I asked, my manhood and pride getting the best of me.

"Don't, Seth! Can we talk about something else, please."

When she didn't answer, I knew. He was better than me.

"Seth, all that doesn't matter anymore. Can we put Kelly out of our house, so we can talk like adults? Look at me, babe. I'm hurting, I'm starving, and I'm scared." She cried. "You don't have to worry about Gianni, anymore. Didn't you say he's dead?"

I thought about letting her go. But could I really trust her that she wouldn't tell the police? Nah, first time's on me, there won't be a second. I stared at her as I bit into the apple. "Gianni's not dead. He's very much alive. But him being alive shouldn't mean anything to you, right? You said you don't love him anymore." I took another bite from the apple before tossing the rest to her.

"Enjoy, it may be your last!"

# Kingpen

## Chapter 15

### Eastwood

"Eastwood!"

I flinched as Archie called my name. Ever since the incident in the shower, I've been on the edge. I was in here for murder. But stabbing someone was way worse than shooting someone. I didn't feel no type of remorse for them bitch ass niggas that tried to take Hotboy out the game. They deserved everything that they got. You know what, I take that back. I wish I would've done them niggas som' nasty. I should've hung their naked bodies up in the shower, so that everyone could see.

"What! My nigga, I'ma tell you this one time, and one time only. Don't sneak up on me like that ever again. This is the penitentiary, not the playground."

Archie nodded. Being only twenty-one years old, Archie didn't take the penitentiary serious. No kid did. He was an adult, but to the penitentiary, he was a baby. Looking at his pale skin, you couldn't tell what race he was. When he pulled up on the unit, he had everyone confused. He claimed his Mexican side and shamed the white side. He was beyond bad as hell. He was playful as hell too. He wasn't afraid to get his hands dirty, if he had to. In his heart, Archie wasn't Mexican, or white. He was all nigga.

"My bad, blood. I fucked up," he said, putting his hands up to slap box. Archie wasn't a homie yet. But he was a bounty hunter at heart, and he was always ready to show it.

"Keep putting yo' hands up at me, and I'ma show you, you ain't ready." I toyed with him: I kept a straight face, pretending I was serious.

"So, what's the move, big homie?" Archie asked.

We stood outside the dayroom as Sanderfield walked on the wing. She looked tired, like she had been here all night. I watched her as she relieved the other C.O. "The move is, to move without being seen—That's the move," I said.

"No, shit!" Archie spat. "I'm saying, I need to get in the mix. I need to make some bread to pay for this appeal lawyer. Bitch ass nigga talking about he want twenty stacks, just to consider my case. That's a lot, but he's the best in the business. He got a ninety-five percent rate on appeals."

Sanderfield looked at me and Archie as the other C.O. left to go home. She looked at both of us, but her eyes lingered on me longer. She looked me up and down, then she walked in the closet. "Twenty stacks ain't bad for yo' freedom. Especially with the kind of case you got." I thought about my own appeal. My lawyer wanted thirty thousand for my freedom; that's what I'm gon' give him. How? By any means necessary.

"It ain't a lot—But how the fuck am I gon' get twenty stacks, I'm in here," Archie said.

"Plenty ways, lil' homie. What about yo' parents, or yo' girl?" I pointed out.

"My girl, Rosa, she's down by law. She's been working overtime every day, just to get the money for the lawyer." He sighed. "My parents, they're in prison, too."

Sanderfield walked out the closet and looked at me again. A small smile came across her face, then it disappeared as quickly as it came.

"What you mean, yo' parents locked up, too? Mama and daddy?" I asked, curious. I always thought that black people were the ones that dealt with the history of their moms and daddies passing the curse down for their kids to come to prison. I guess blacks and whites do have a few things in common.

"Yea', both of them are in prison. My mom, she's about to see parole soon. My dad, he got a fifteen-year sentence. He comes up for parole in a few years."

"Why?" I asked

"Because—because—of me," he answered with sorrow.

"Of you? Wait, what? Stop with the dramatic ass shit and tell me what happened.

"They got locked up for aggravated robbery. My mama and daddy went on a robbery spree to get enough money to buy me a lawyer."

I shook my head. I felt sorry for his entire family, but I had to salute his mom and pops. They went all out to get him not to go to prison. In the end, the system always wins. "Damn, homie. I'm sorry to hear that. I hope all is well with them. When you get out, make sure you do the right thing. You at least owe them that." Sanderfield walked out the closet. She looked at me, her eyes told me to come here.

"Yea', I know," Archie agreed. "I'ma do what I can to take care of them when I get out. That's overstood." He was clueless as to what I really meant.

"Doing right by them has nothing to do with money," I said.

He looked at me like I had a bugger in my nose. "So how am I supposed to repay them?" he asked.

"By not coming back to prison once you finally get out."

I left him with that to think about. Sanderfield watched me as I walked over to her. She had put her hair up in a ponytail, with the end curly. She must've went in the closet and put some make-up on. She had some strawberry lip gloss and some eye shadow on. The lip gloss made her lips look juicy as hell. "What's up? You okay?" I asked her.

She put her left hand in her back pocket, and popped her legs, making herself look bowlegged. "Yea', I'm okay—Just tired," she answered.

"Why you tired? You just got here."

"Actually, I've been here since last night. I'm working a double. Today's my Friday." She sounded excited.

"Oh, yeah. Freaky Friday, huh? What you gon' do on

yo' days off?" I asked.

She shifted her weight, making her hips pop out. I had to admit, she was bad, for a penitentiary bitch. "Me and my girls are going to go to Dallas. Meek Mills is supposed to perform live."

"That's what's up," I said. "What you planning on wearing? You can't go to Dallas live, wearing just anything. You got to put on for East Texas."

She smirked and said, "Trust, I'm gon' turn some heads. I got this red, Fendi dress that I just bought. I guarantee a boss nigga is gon' see me and will want to pay me to get me out of it." She spoke like she had done it before.

"So, you doing it like that?" I said. "So, how much will it cost to get you out this uniform?" I boldly asked. I caught her by surprise, but the fuse had already been lit. There was no turning back now.

Before she could respond, a cock blocker called my name.

"Eastwood!" an inmate yelled outside the main gate.

I heard him, but I didn't answer. Sanderfield looked at me, then at the inmate on the door. "Eastwood!" the inmate yelled my name again. I felt like Ice Cube, on the movie, '*Friday After Next*', when Day Day walked in on Craig and Donna.

"Someone's at the door for you," Sanderfield said, like I didn't already know.

"'Give me a sec," I told her before I walked to see what the fuck he wanted. I walked up to the gate, heated. "My nigga, what the fuck you want? Calling my name like that!" I spat. I knew the guy, but I didn't know him familiarly. I knew him from around the way.

"My bad, bruh—I got this kite," he said, as he pulled a folded-up piece of paper from out the corner of his jaw. He had the paper tucked inside a rubber glove, for protection. "Vetta Vuchii told me to give this to you. He said it needs to be taken care of, like yesterday."

I grabbed the kite, balled it up in my hand, and walked away. I couldn't argue with him, seeing that the kite came from the big homie, Vetta Vuchii.

Vetta Vuchii was the big homie on the unit. Not just the unit, but also from the world. Vuchii was known all throughout Fort Worth, for banging that five. He had put in his work with the Pirus since he was a teenager, when the Pirus first came to Texas. Vuchii went from foot soldier to G-status, before the age of twenty-five. Vuchii was known for his murder game. He had a double life sentence for two murders that he had committed all for the love of the five. That didn't stop him, though. Even from behind the concrete, he still was a shot caller. What Vuchii said, went!

Sanderfield looked at me as I walked away from the door. "So, where were we?" I asked her.

"You ain't slick!" Sanderfield spat.

I balled my fist up tighter, hoping she wouldn't ask what was in my hand. "What? Why you say that?" I hope she didn't push the issue.

She looked at my balled-up fist. I knew then that she saw the whole play. If push came to shove, I was going to have to do what I had to do to make sure she didn't get the kite from me. There was no telling what the kite said.

Sanderfield shook her head and said. "Just know, you ain't slick." She walked off. "Get rid of it before I come back, or I'ma have to do what they pay me to do." She walked away to do her security check.

I walked in the janitor's closet and took the kite out of the rubber glove. I turned the sink on, just in case someone walked up, I could easily drop the kite in the drain, and let the water wash it away. *Whatever's on this kite better be important*, I thought, as I unfolded the paper.

As I read the beginning of the kite, my jaw dropped. "What—the fuck!"

# Kingpen

\*\*\*

## Hotboy

"Wake up, bitch! Come downstairs, the homies holding a ten-ninety. Right now." Eastwood woke me up, like the world was ending. I looked at my clock. Damn, I'd slept all the way to lunch time. I rarely slept that late. Good pussy will drain the life out of a nigga.

"Who called the meeting?" I asked, as I got ready.

"Vuchii. He called the meeting. He shot a kite, it's 9-1-1!"

Vuchii rarely called a mandatory ten-ninety. Especially through a kite. So, whatever it was, it had to be serious. Even though I'm a Vicelord, and they're bloods, I still went to their meetings, off the strength that we all are allies. The bloods held me down when trouble came my way, and vice versa.

"Did Vuchii say what the meeting was about?" I asked as I spat toothpaste in the toilet.

Eastwood looked at me, like he didn't want to say. He sighed and said, "It's—it's about—you!"

I stood at the blood table, along with ten other homies. The dayroom was packed. Everyone in the dayroom was happy that we didn't go on lockdown for that corona virus shit. Even though there was two TV's in the dayroom, all eyes were on us. I stood with my back against the wall as the rest of the homies surrounded the table.

I had been the only homie that wasn't in the dayroom when the news came. So, all the other homies knew already what the meeting was about. I was the only one in the blind. Whenever we held a meeting, it was never good. Either someone was about to get violated or smashed out. We never had any positive meetings. I never understood the point of having opps, when we were always at each other's necks.

Eastwood addressed the pound. "What's popping, y'all? This is a mandatory meeting. So, whoever's not here will be getting a violation." We all looked around the circle, to see who wasn't in attendance. Only one person wasn't present, and that was Lil' Nine. Being that Lil' Nine was in school, he would be given a pass. In attendance was: me, Eastwood, B-Crazy, Los, Lil' Deun, Florida, JayJay, Archie, Divine, and Lil' Nip.

The only person that looked out of place was B-Crazy. B-Crazy was a white boy that looked like he should've been working on Wall Street. B-Crazy had been in prison for over twenty-five years. He was a B.S.V. (Blood Stone Villain). He had some slick black hair, like an Italian. He wore glasses that sometimes fooled niggas into thinking he was some geeky white boy pretending to be tough. B-Crazy had been repping in the pen', when bloods were outnumbered two to one, by the crips. Today, he's a penitentiary legend. One of the only white bloods to survive in prison, during the time when being white, and being a white blood, didn't bring any benefits. Even now, he still bangs like he just got put down.

"Y'all want to do roll call?" Eastwood asked the table. "We got two new homies, so B-Crazy, if you want to start—"

B-Crazy leaned over the table. "Yeah, I gotcha. He looked around the table at all the homies. We were small in numbers, but we had some heavy hitters. "I'm B-Crazy, G-Status, Blood Stone Villain." B-Crazy spoke as he shook up with the homies around the table.

My patience was growing thin. Here we were, shaking hands, and shit. I didn't feel like shaking hands, or hearing about no nigga set. The only thing I wanted to hear was, why the fuck we were holding this meeting about me!

"Lil' Nip, Five Nine, Piru," Lil' Nip said, as he started shaking all the homies' hands. When he got to me, I refused to shake his hand. I didn't mean any disrespect, I just wasn't feeling this shit at all. We could've saved all this friendly shit till afterwards.

"My nigga!" I said, agitated. "Why the fuck are we here? We can do all this shit later. Let's get down to business. I needed a cigarette badly.

Lil' Nip looked at me like he was fucked up about something. I didn't give two fucks. Nip was a lil' homie. He was new on the scene; I didn't owe him any explanation. I was glad that I had my banger on me. I knew when Eastwood said the meeting was about me, it was gon' be about som' straight bullshit. Ever since the incident in the shower, I never left my cell without a shank. I'd rather get caught with it, than get caught without it.

"Look out, Hotboy! I feel you, but you owe the lil' homie an apology," B-Crazy said. "Shake up with him, then we can get to the point at hand."

Lil' Nip folded his arms. I held my hand out for him to shake. Nip looked at me for a brief second, then he locked the five with me, then he crossed his arms again, obviously in his feelings.

"Now what's up? Why are we here?" I asked, ready to get this shit over with.

"We got a kite from the big homie on the north side," Eastwood spoke. "Vuchii said some crip niggas pulled up on him in the chow hall. They told him, if he don't run you off, then it's gon' be a war, one we can't win."

"Wait a minute! Som' crip niggas! So, you telling me we having a meeting about som' opps. Fuck them niggas, dog!" Los ranted. "If they want war, then we bring it to them!" he added. I knew whatever the issue was, Los and Eastwood would ride with me, fo' sure.

B-Crazy spoke up. "It's more to it. Look, five, I'ma come out and say it. Them crab ass niggas throwing dirt on yo' name. They saying you snitched on Uncle Marvin."

I looked at Crazy as he spoke. I couldn't help but laugh

on the inside. Niggas was trying every route to get me out the way. That's how I knew I was on my best shit. "My nigga! Y'all fo' real right now. That's what this shit is all about, some rumors. Y'all got to be kidding me, homie." I was getting more and more agitated.

"Nigga, that ain't no small issue. Vuchii said, if you don't make it right, then you have to go!" B-Crazy spat.

I had mad love for B-Crazy. He had gave me a lot of insight on the penitentiary game when I first pulled up. I knew this shit wasn't personal with him. He was just a blood down to the heart, he was just following orders.

"Run me off! Crazy, how long have you been knowing me?" I asked. Not waiting on an answer, I said, "You know, I'm not going anywhere. By force, or by choice! "I stuck my right hand in my pants, gripping the handle to the shank. I wanted one of them niggas to feel froggy. My body count was gon' climb like a skinny bitch on a stair master.

Crazy mean-mugged me. He wasn't buying that gangsta shit I was spitting. Shid, he was a gangsta too. He had been killing niggas before I was even born. "If you don't plan on going anywhere, then you better get to talking!" B-Crazy said, folding his arms.

I knew every homie was ready to jump at the sound of Crazy's voice. I was outnumbered. Even with Los and Eastwood. "I can't believe this shit! Y'all know what. When this is all over with, I'm sliding back. Weak ass shit!" I spat furiously. "I never told y'all before, but Uncle Marvin took the case for me. When we were cellys, the laws found a banger and a pound of K2 under the toilet." I sighed. I couldn't believe I was snitching on myself. The game had definitely changed. "The laws locked us both up." I continued, "Until they figured out whose shit it was. In the beginning, I planned on taking my own rap. It took me som' time, because I didn't want to snitch on myself, but, I thought about Unc'." I paused and looked around the table. Once the smoke finally cleared, shit would never be the same. The niggas that I had placed above my family now looked at me as the enemy. I had placed my life and my freedom on the line numerous times for them. I proved my loyalty to them from day one. Look where that got me, under the gun. "Me and Unc' were in segregation. We spoke throughout the vent. He told me that he would take the rap for me. He knew with the life sentence he already had, he wouldn't see the free world again, so we did a pump fake. I ended up taking it to trial. Uncle Marvin got on the stand. He admitted to everything, saying he was the one that had everything. They ended up giving him another life sentence stacked on top of the one he already had. Like it mattered. They let me go, 'cause they had to. I didn't snitch on no one."

I felt like a hypocrite, exposing my hand, to save my character. I couldn't read Eastwood's face to see if he believed me or not. B-Crazy stared at me. I knew he was just trying to make me sweat. Even during a workout, I never sweated.

In a deeply serious tone, B-Crazy said: "If anyone has anything to say, then now is the time. Because when the meeting is over, there shouldn't be shit said behind anyone's back. This meeting isn't just about Hotboy. If you niggas got anything on y'alls chest, about anything, or anybody, now is the time to get it off." B-Crazy's presence alone made most niggas tremble. All the homies stood in silence. I knew deep down, some of the homies wanted to say something, but they feared the repercussions. I wasn't a big homie like B-Crazy, or Vuchii, but I did earn my respect the same way they did. I never backed down from no nigga, and I wasn't afraid to send a nigga to see his maker.

Lil' Nip fidgeted, like he wanted to say something. I guess he bought some balls from commissary, 'cause he actually found the nerve to speak up. "I don't really know what's the situation on Hotboy's issue. I just pulled up, so

I don't know how close you and Uncle Marvin were." Nip never looked me in my eyes. He stared at the table, and said, "I got som' else on my mind. I know a lot of homies feel the same way, they just don't want to say nothing."
I looked at each homie around the table. Neither of them could look me in the face—except Crazy, Los, and Eastwood. "Well, since they can't talk, you say it for 'em," I said, showing my anger. I gave Nip the boost he needed to speak his mind.
"The homies feel like y'all ain't packing fair." Nip looked at me, Los, and Eastwood. "The homies feel like you, Eastwood, and Los, treating us like dope fiends, instead of homies."
I wanted to reach across the table and slap the shit out of the lil' nigga. They didn't comprehend what we had to go through to get what we had. All the stress a nigga had to endure. Always wondering when the laws were going to shake the spot down. Selfish ass niggas, talking like we didn't bless every homie every time the pack came in. It might've not been what they wanted, but it was enough for them to put some food in their lockers.
"My nigga!" Los said. "Fuck all that shit you talkin' 'bout, that's on third ward, y'all niggas on som' straight bitch shit!"
"Who else? If it ain't just you, then who else feel like we ain't packing fair?" Eastwood asked.
Lil' Nip stayed silent. He looked around at a few homies. One being Divine. Divine never liked me. He never said anything to me personally, but I could tell by his body language every time I came into the room. Whenever I was around, Divine would walk off, or sit far away from me. He was one of those silent haters, always hissing his tongue like a snake.
"I feel the same way," Divine spoke up. "Well, not towards Los, and Eastwood. Hotboy, you don't ever pack fair. You walk around like I'm yo' enemy, or som'."

I laughed in his face. "My nigga! What is this? Child support court? Y'all acting like some straight-up bitches! Hotboy ain't do this, Hotboy ain't do that!" I said, mimicking a girl. "A nigga don't owe y'all niggas shit, homie. I'm a Vicelord." I patted my chest. "I aid and assist. Everything else is a blessing. Truthfully, I'm supposed to aid and assist, only if y'all are outnumbered. Fuck all that other friendly shit! I am the five, you niggas just under it! Neither of you niggas put in a dollar for the drop to come in. But y'all want to reap the benefits. You niggas some characters!" I was heated. I really felt like doing some punching. With whoever! I was a fool with a banger, but I was lethal from the shoulders, and they knew it, too. I took my shirt off, leaving my wife beater on. I was hot, but I knew, in the back of their minds, they thought I was ready to take it there.

B-Crazy stood beside Florida, with his arms crossed. I just knew he was about to vote me off the island, with the performance I just displayed for the entire dayroom to see. "If y'all through putting on a show for the dayroom, then we can get this shit over with," B-Crazy said. "The homie, Hotboy, is right. He don't owe y'all nothing, or me either. He went out on the limb to get what he got. Y'all can do the same thing. Neither does Los or Eastwood owe y'all shit. Y'all supposed to aid and assist, because of ya' love you got for the five, not 'cause what the next nigga got, or what he do for you." B-Crazy looked me right in the eyes. "You said when the smoke clears, you're sliding back. Is that how you really feel?" Crazy asked.

I crossed my arms and said, "Said that, meant that!"

B-Crazy mugged me. I knew he felt like I'd stabbed him in the back. He always told me that he hated when homies slid back. I didn't have a choice. They had stacked the deck and forced my hand. It was either fold or lose everything in one wop.

"Say no mo'! You on yo' own then!" B-Crazy spat.

"Don't call on us, when them crip niggas come at cha. Like you said, *said that, meant that!*"

I looked around the table. The same niggas that I stood on the front line with was now just like an opposition. 'Cause if you weren't with me, you was against me. I didn't give two fucks. I could do bad all by myself.

I walked off from the meeting. Fuck their roll call, and whatever else they had in mind. Now I knew I was alone, and who was gunning for me. All I had to do was, watch my own back. To hell with a homie!

# Kingpen

## Chapter 16

### Lakewood

I pulled up to Kiles' house. I dialed his number. "Aye! I'm outside," I spoke into the phone.

I don't know what Hotboy got going on. He knew Kiles had som' type of relationship to Gabby, yet he still wanted to do business with him. Whatever he had going on, I wasn't feeling it at all! First, Hotboy had me tail Kiles. Come to find out, the white boy is a straight killa. Now, he had me dropping work off to the damn fool, at his house.

He stood at the front door of his house. Kiles waved me over. I stepped out the car, and walked over to him with a Nike shopping bag in my hand. "Kiles, right?" I said, pretending to not already know.

Kiles sat down, then gestured for me to sit in the lawn chair beside him. "Yea, I'm Kiles," he said. "Is that it?" he asked, reaching for the bag.

I sat down in the lawn chair and held my hand out for him to shake. We were in a nice suburban neighborhood. I figured a few of his neighbors probably had those door cameras. If they did, I wanted them to see us having a normal conversation, not a drug transaction. "Shake my hand," I said, sitting the bag on the concrete. Once he shook my hand, I explained why I did what I did.

"Oh, I see," he said. "But, I don't have nosey neighbors. We stay to ourselves."

I laughed on the inside. There was some truth to what he said. No one saw me the day I broke into his house, so maybe they weren't nosey. "Safety precautions. You never know who's watching you!" I said.

"Yea, I know what you mean. So, what's up? What you got for me?" he asked.

He looked like he was high. My instinct told me not to give him the work. I could smell dope coming out of his pores. I promised Hotboy I would, so I had to. I was a man of my word; I couldn't let him down.

"It's a half a pound of K2. A zip of ice, and five hundred X.O.'s. Make sure he gets it all."

"No doubt! I'll get it to him. Matter of fact, I'll take it to him later. I got a lil' over an hour before I have to go to work. I'll take it inside, and get it wrapped up and ready." Kiles kept peeping at the bag. I knew as soon as he went inside, he was going to pinch out of everything, except the pills, only because they're accounted for.

"*Thunp!*" A loud thump came from a small basement window not too far from where we were sitting. The sound caused us both to look in the direction of the small window. "What was that? —Did you hear that?—Sounded like someone threw a rock at yo' window," I said.

Kiles stood up and grabbed the Nike bag. "That's probably my son—I bought him a ping pong table—All he knows how to do is, spike the balls," he said, looking at the window. "I told his badass to be careful, or he's going to break a window." Kiles stepped to the front door with the bag in his hand. "I'll be sure to get this to Kingsley today. Okay, bye!" He rushed inside and slammed the door behind him.

I shook my head and laughed. His son was in for a rude awakening. White people and their weird lives! Truthfully, they were just as bad off as black folks; they just had a better way at hiding it. I stood up from the lawn chair and stretched. I looked at my watch. I still had a little over forty-five minutes until Mama Dee got off work. That old pussy was so good and tight. I couldn't get enough of her.

I took a step off the porch and stopped. I looked around back and forth. I could've sworn I heard someone call my name. I took another step, then I heard it again. This time, it wasn't as faint as the first time. I didn't know anyone in the neighborhood, so who in the hell was calling my name? I pulled out my phone to make sure I didn't do a butt dial. I had to be tripping. Then again, every time I didn't smoke weed, I'll start tripping, thinking som' crazy shit. It's been a lil' over an hour; that's way too long.

I stuck my finger in my ear as I heard my name again. I shook my head and walked to my car. "Damn, I gotta stop smoking!"

\*\*\*

### Newton

"Oh—my—God! Uhmm!" I moaned as I bit into the apple that Seth gave me. Even as I bit into the apple, my stomach still growled. I hadn't ate in over a week. Now I knew how homeless people felt. I ate the apple down to the core and seeds. I tried to move my legs. Sitting down for so long made my whole body feel numb.

I looked around the basement. I hadn't been down here, but to only wash clothes. It was crazy, because Seth was against the idea of having a basement when we were about to rent this house. He said something about the property tax being higher because of the basement. I ended up talking him into getting it. Now I wish I'd just kept my mouth closed.

I jumped as I heard the sound of a car door slamming. Maybe it was Seth on his way to work. Once I didn't hear the engine come to life, I knew it had to be a visitor. It was only a matter of time before someone showed up. My mom hadn't heard from me since the day me and Seth got into it. I knew sooner or later, she would ask about me. Then I thought the worse. *What if Seth does something to her? What if he hits her, shoot her, or worse—kill her*! Then I heard faint sounds of a man's voice. I recognized Seth's voice, but I couldn't make out the other guy's voice.

"Arghh!" I groaned, as I attempted to scoot closer to the window. I looked at my leg. The blood had finally dried up around the bone. The flesh around the blood had begun to smell. I couldn't feel my leg, but the pain reminded me it was still there, every time I tried to move.

I cupped my ear with one hand to try to hear better. I could hear Seth and another man conversing back and forth on the porch. They were actually doing a drug transaction on our front porch. I sat there and eavesdropped on their conversation. The other guy's voice sounded so familiar. I felt like I knew him, but I couldn't put a face with his voice. I thought as hard as I could. The voice reminded me of Gianni, for some odd reason. It took me back to the first day when I worked on Gianni's wing with Mama Dee, and Williamson. Gianni's friend had tried his best to get at Mama Dee. He did make her smile, though. Lakewood was his name, I recalled.

"Lakewood!" I said to myself. Then again, why was he here doing a drug deal with Seth? Was Lakewood in on all of this? Nah, he couldn't have been. Seth had said that Gianni was dead. Then again, he later came back and said he wasn't dead. I had to take my chances. I didn't want to die, and especially down here, alone.

"Lakewood!" I shouted to the top of my lungs. I couldn't tell if he heard me through Seth's deep voice. I looked around for something, anything. A rock, a shoe, anything to make a loud noise with. I took my shoe off. Thankfully, only one of them had flew off when I fell down the stairs. I clutched the shoe with a tight grip. I threw it as hard as I could. As the shoe flew, I sent a prayer to God asking him to perfect my aim. "Yes!" I said, as the shoe connected with the window, making a loud thumping noise.

I wasn't able to see out the window from where I was sitting, but I knew that whatever they were talking about had come to a halt. It was quiet for a second, then they resumed talking again. The front door slammed. It had to be Seth coming to shut me up. The way the door slammed could only mean one thing. They heard me. I could hear footsteps moving above my head, fast.

"Lakewood!" I shouted. The footsteps came closer. "Lakewood!" I shouted, with tears falling down my face.

Seth opened the basement door. He ran down the stairs with his gun in his hand. Anger plastered all over his face. I looked at him with tears in my eyes.

Seth raised his gun, and came down hard on my head, knocking me unconscious.

# Kingpen

# Chapter 17

### Hotboy

"Where you finna go, bitch?" Eastwood asked me, as I stood by the main gate. I wasn't dressed in my normal starched whites. I was dressed in some normal, regular whites, with some old New Balances on. My shank was tucked inside my waistband.

"I'm about to go and clear my name," I said. "I can't be walking around with that kind of jacket on my back. I'm too playa to be a motherfucking snitch!" My feelings were on my sleeve. Niggas had crossed me in the worse way. If the rumor got around, I could get crossed out. I wasn't afraid of what another nigga had planned for me. I was a killa, too. My concern was no one wanted to do business with a snitch. Knowing Beto, the word was already out.

"You wasn't gon' tell me?" Eastwood sounded upset. "My nigga, fuck what them niggas was talkin' 'bout at the ten-ninety. I'ma Eastwood Piru! Niggas ain't got no say-so over me. My big homie in the free world. I know you ain't no snitch. We just bodied two niggas together. So, whatever you planning on doing, I'm riding."

That was why Eastwood was my nigga. Since Lakewood had went home, Eastwood and I had grown closer. Even before, he was my homie. Now though, we're closer than ever.

"My nigga, I might have to catch another body— Somebody has to answer for this shit, homie," I said.

Eastwood stepped closer to me and said, "I didn't have any problems catching a body with you before. So let's get down to business."

I laughed. Eastwood was the definition of a real nigga. "Fuck it! Let's shake the unit up," I said.

"All chow, head to the north chow hall!" the Lt. yelled, as me and Eastwood moved past the line. I noticed B-wing in the chow hall eating as we walked past the south chow

119

hall. We weren't allowed to eat with the sex offenders.

As soon as we walked in the north chow hall, I started sweating. The chow hall was packed. The north side of the unit was considered the hood—the projects. It was easy as hell to get inside the north chow hall, but even harder to get out. The C.O.'s would cram us in and make us wait an hour just to get out. Like always, there was only one male C.O. in the chow hall. If we wanted to be on som' hoe ass nigga shit, we could've smashed the C.O., and get away with it, because the chow hall didn't have any cameras.

"What's popping, bitch!" T-man said, as he spotted me amongst the crowd. T-man stood with Major and another homie by the name of Cory D. Cory D was a homie from Dallas. He was always into some shit. He was known for fighting and banging. He had a special style of fighting. It was called, 'taking off'. He didn't care if his opponent was ready or not. If he felt threatened, or disrespected, he would take off on you, every time.

I embraced the homies, as we took over three tables. Instead of sitting on the seats, we sat on top of the table.

"So, what's up?" Major asked. "I heard the fake news." He laughed.

I figured the rumor had already got out. Beto should've been a woman's prison, 'cause the niggas here gossiped like bitches. "I'm looking for them niggas right now. That's why I came to chow. You know I ain't gon' let that shit slide. That's on the big five!" I said. I looked around the chow hall for one of the level-headed crip niggas. Even though I was in my feelings, I was due to see parole any day. All the same, I had murder on my mind; don't get me wrong. But I still had to move smart. I'd be damned if I spent the rest of my life in here. I had to be the out of the group with a level head. I was with some gorillas. They wouldn't hesitate to pop shit off, and deal with the consequences later.

"Them niggas was in here a minute ago—I just saw

Trill and his homies in the line, waiting to get their trays," Cory said.

I went into killa mode. Trill was the one that told Vuchii about the fake news. Trill was Dame's homie. I was surprised they weren't together the night I killed Dame.

Major looked at me and smiled. I already knew what was on his mind. He lived for that gangsta shit. T-Man, too! Eastwood stood beside me, quiet as hell. I knew I didn't have to question him when it was go time. He had already showed me that he was about that life.

"I'm just gon' holla at the nigga—If he talkin' right, then everything is everything," I said. Major, Cory D, and T-Man were all cheesing. "Look at y'all niggas. Always ready to pop som' shit off." I laughed.

The four of us walked in Trill's direction. Trill was laughing with his homies, until he looked over and saw me. Trill knew, like I knew, that he had fucked up, and put the wrong nigga name in his mouth. He thought he could spread a rumor about me, hoping my homies would've ran me off by now. Wrong idea!

Trill looked at his homies, who were in line with him. Trill ducked under the rail and walked over to us with his homies in tow. I led them to the far end of the chow hall, a distance away from the lonely C.O., and away from the neutrons. I wanted to be able to see who was *who*, just in case shit popped off.

"Whats cracking?" Trill taunted, making Major sigh. I knew Major wanted to pop shit off. I looked at Major, hoping he could read my expression. As bad as I wanted to take off on Trill, I needed to know exactly what he knew.

"Ain't shit cracking! What's up, why you got my name in yo' mouth?"

"'Cause you a rat, and all rats got to die!"

Trill's homies thought that shit was funny.

Los must've noticed us. He walked up and joined the party. "What's popping?" Los greeted me. "These the niggas?" Los asked.

"Yea', this the nigga—I'm tryna see who put him up to it, to even say I'ma snitch," I said to Los, but loud enough for everyone to hear. "Somebody had to pay him, 'cause we all know he ain't no real gangsta to do it on his own," I said. I looked at Trill and said, "So what's up, clown? Who paid you to perform all these tricks?"

Trill's homie—Crazy-Cuz—moved behind him like he wanted to do some damage. Crazy-Cuz was known for taking niggas dope and robbing the C.O.'s when they came to work with a pack on them. Crazy-Cuz made his name when he knocked a nigga named D-Bo out. D-Bo was supposed to be live from the shoulders. Crazy-Cuz knocked him out by mistake, if you ask me. Swinging with his head down and his eyes closed, like a straight broad!

"You a'ight, homie?" Cory addressed Crazy-Cuz. "You got som' frog in you? —Over there flinching and shit," Cory D said.

I could tell that shit was about to go south. This was the perfect time, and the perfect place. The only thing I was considering was my parole. One fuck up could set me off. That was something I couldn't deal with.

"Who you calling a clown?" Trill shot back. "Say, cuz, you got the game fucked up. I ain't Dame! I already know you the one that did the homie dirty. Fucking with me, you got another thing coming."

"But you calling me a snitch! My nigga, I ain't have nothing to do with yo' homie gettin' hit up. What I'm tryna do is, prevent you from ending up the same way."

Trill wasn't as gangsta as he was pretending to be. He knew that the real gangstas was the ones standing in front of him. He had to play the gangsta role in front of his homies. That type of shit got a lot of niggas sent to a pine box. Especially fucking with me.

"You already know what it is!" Trill said.

I couldn't take it anymore. I tried being civilized,

despite the disrespect he kept shooting at me. It's like he knew I was waiting to see parole, 'cause he knew I was about that action.

T-Man walked off from the group. He went through a crowd of inmates, then I couldn't see him anymore.

"So, what you wanna do?" Trill said on another level. "Even though you said you ain't dead the homie, I still feel like you did! So, whatever you wanna do, I'ma match it!" Trill hyped himself up.

T-Man came through the crowd, from behind Trill and his homies. His sneaky ass was up to his old tricks. He hit me with the whooptie-blam. I thought fo'sure he had left. I should've known.

T-Man grabbed a pitcher from off a table, holding it by the handle; he cocked it back and came forward, full force, smashing it on the side of Crazy-Cuz's head. The impact made a loud crashing sound. The element of surprise caught Trill and his homies off guard. I was on Trill before it could register in his head. I hit him with a jab so fast. He tried to run and tripped over Crazy-Cuz's feet. Crazy-Cuz was laid out on the floor, snoring. Blood was gushing out his head. Trill looked back at me from the ground with pleading eyes. I knew he was a straight bitch.

Cory D snatched another one of Trill's homies up and dunked him on his back. The nigga had the nerve to start swinging from the ground, on som' MMA type shit. Major was in a full-fledged boxing match with another random crip that had come to help once he saw his homies fighting. They were throwing nothing but heat. There was no bobbing, or weaving, just straight haymakers.

The chow hall was so loud. In the beginning, people didn't know what the fuck was going on. As they started watching Major and the crip nigga fight, everything registered. Before I knew it, every blood, and crip in the chow hall had started fighting each other. The C.O. panicked and picked up his walkie-talkie. He raised it to his lips. Before he could say anything, a Mexican blindsided him, rocking him right to sleep.

Me and Trill were going at it for a minute, until he tried som' stupid shit that he must've seen on a movie. Trill squatted low, as he tried to sweep my leg up. I hadn't seen that shit since I was a teenager. That was som' straight Dallas shit. I saw the move coming as soon as he squatted. I scooped him up with a badass uppercut. He fell backwards, hitting his head on a steel seat. T-Man was on him as soon as his body dropped. T-Man stomped him like Chris Spencer did in the movie, *'Don't Be a Menace to South Central While Drinking Your Juice in the Hood.'* All around the chow hall, niggas were throwing blows. Some people didn't even know why they were fighting; they just were. My throat began to itch, out of nowhere. My breathing became harsh, then my eyes started watering. People that were fighting started coughing slowly. A couple of inmates closer to the chow hall door started vomiting. That's when I saw the black suit team with riot gear and shields. They shot gas can after gas can at us.

"Pull up, bitch!" I shouted to T-Man, who was helping Cory D jump som' fool. I snatched Major up, as well as Los. I looked around, but I couldn't find Eastwood. "You see Eastwood?" I asked T-Man, as I looked around the chow hall. T-Man pointed to a corner behind us. Eastwood was engaged in a full-fledged boxing match with a Hispanic. I couldn't figure out how that even began. T-Man ran over and snuck the Hispanic from behind. The blow didn't knock him out, but it did set up the punch for Eastwood to knock him out.

"Hoe ass nigga!" Eastwood spat. "Nigga snuck me from behind." Eastwood covered his face with his shirt.

I laughed and said, "My nigga, you the only one fighting a Hispanic, what the fuck!" I teased.

Eastwood held up his hand, as he tried to catch his breath. "That nigga—" he panted. "He's a crip—That was

Ese," Eastwood said.

Ese was a known Hispanic crip. He was ten toes down when it came to cripping.

"Get on the fucking ground! Put your fucking hands behind your heads!" the head warden yelled behind a bullhorn, from a safe distance, with a lot of backup.

"Fuck what he talkin' 'bout, blood," Major said, looking down. "This flo' dirty as hell," he said.

"Dog, get down, or them hoes gon' lay you down," Eastwood told him. "Them hoes will kill you, ain't no cameras in here, fam'," Eastwood said, as he kneeled down.

I came here prepared. I knew shit was gon' get ugly. That's why I didn't wear my whites. I took my shank out of my waistband and slid it across the floor. I had a feeling they'll search us one by one. I shook my head. I had just made that bitch; now I had to make another one.

I kneeled down as I looked for a spot that wasn't too dirty. I found a spot beside Major, who was sitting on his ass, instead of lying on his stomach, like we were supposed to do. I laughed at him. He didn't give a fuck. Major looked at me and laughed. "Fuck the police!"

\*\*\*

## Seth

The sergeant waved us through as we waited in line to get searched. "Just come on through, we don't have time to search today. There is an I.C.S. going on in the north chow hall."

I walked past the sergeant and thanked God. I was packed down today. I got high before work, so when it was time for me to get ready to come to work, I had forgot to wrap Kingsley's pack. I was running late already, so I only had enough time to get dressed. Instead of vacuum-sealing the pack, like I usually did. I just wrapped it in duct tape. It helped a little.

I ran down the hallway to the north end. The head warden had ceased all movement, in order to get the chow hall cleared out. There were half naked inmates lined up all down the hallway. The inmates sat on the floor, legs crossed, with their hands zip-tied behind their backs. That had to be one badass riot. I wish I could've watched it.

"Kiles!" Sergeant Childs called my name. "Come with me!" she ordered, as she ran past me without telling me where we were going. Sergeant Childs was a short, sexy Caucasian woman, who was country as they came. She stood at 5'5, 120lbs, all ass and hips. All she ever did was, run around the unit at full speed. You could tell she loved her job more than she should. She was down to earth, and a people person. I had her on my to-fuck list. I knew if I could catch her one day after work, I could easily get her to ride me like a bull.

I lightly jogged behind her, watching her ass bounce with every step she took. Damn, she's fine. She finally stopped in front of X-wing's door. X-wing was used for investigation purposes. Each cell held one inmate.

Sergeant Childs went on: "Once we find out how many cells we have available, we'll start moving all the inmates with blood on their hands and clothes. If they look like they were a part of the riot, then they're going to X-wing."

I was listening, but at the same time, I was trying to catch my breath. Sergeant Childs stood in front of me like the long run down the hallway didn't bother her. Sergeant Childs took the lead, which was my pleasure. She had a better body than Gabby and Kelly, so I was enjoying the view.

Sergeant Childs looked at a chart, and scrolled down the entire list. "Let him out," she pointed. "Him, and him, and these two. I'll have them another house in a minute, but right now, I need those cells." The African C.O. she was talking to nodded. Sergeant Childs took off down the hallway again at full speed. I shook my head and chased behind her. *This bitch is sexy*, I thought, *but retarded as hell*. Who in their right mind would run inside a building all day?

"Let me see your hands," I said, to a Hispanic inmate. "Okay, turn around." I looked at his back, for bruises, or scratches. "You're good," I said. He actually had red marks the size of a fist on his back. I wasn't trying to lock anyone up. I was just trying to get this shit over with, so that I could start my shift, and get this pack off of me. All that running I did, chasing after Childs, made the pack slide down. So, now it looked like I had a hard-on. Every time I looked over at Sergeant Childs, she was checking me out. If only she knew what I was really packing.

We cleared the hallway, and still there was inmates filing out of the chow hall. The warden always gave us stupid orders, then he'll walk away, making us do it by ourselves.

"I swear, I ain't been fighting!" Gianni argued with another C.O., who was trying to send him to lock up. "My nigga, you sound dumb than a bitch!" Gianni spat.

I walked over to seize the opportunity. "Let me see your hands," I said to Gianni. He looked up at me. Holding his hands out flat, he showed me his hands, then turned them over. His right hand had a bruise, like he had been in a fight. "You know what—" I said, "I'll take him to X-wing myself." I grabbed Gianni by his zip ties. I placed one hand at the center of his back. I gave him a little shove.

Gianni tried to say something to the sergeant as we walked past. "Shut up!" I spat. "She don't want to talk to you!" I yelled.

I couldn't tell him right then and there, but I was trying to save his ass. Once we finally made it past the north side, I looked around, making sure the coast was clear before I ran into the captain's office. I ran back out with a pair of scissors. "Turn around, before someone sees us," I said, as he faced the wall. I cut the zip ties and tossed them in the trash.

"For a minute, I thought you were going to turn me in," Gianni said, rubbing his wrist.

I had a means to, but that would've been too easy. He'd be out of lockup in a day or two. That wasn't good enough. "Why would I do that?" I asked him.

He eyed me like he wanted to say something. Instead, he just said, "Did you bring the pack?"

That was all he ever thought about. Fucking other people's wives and getting drops. I couldn't wait to finally get rid of him for good. "Yea', I got it. You'll have to watch out for me, while I get it out." He nodded and looked around.

I ran into the captain's office. Luckily, everyone was busy with the riot. I unzipped my pants and took the drop out. I tossed it inside a brown paper bag and folded the top. I peeped my head out the door to make sure the coast was clear. "Come on, scary ass nigga, you good," Gianni said.

I wanted to spit in his face and say to hell with everything. I couldn't, though. In actuality, I was really afraid of him. He was a killer. Me, on the other hand, I had killed. It's a totally different thing. It was easy to kill with a gun. You had to have some major demons, to stab someone to death.

I handed him the johnny sack, with the drop on the inside. "This means, we're good, right? We're square, I don't owe you anymore?"

He nodded. "Yea', we good—I'll text you when this one is almost gone—I'll pay you the usual for the next one," Gianni said.

"I'm done!" I said, causing him to look upset.

"What you mean, you're done? We was just getting started."

I shook my head and said, "I ain't trying to be in here with y'all on this side of the fence. I appreciate everything, but I'm done."

He laughed and said, "My nigga, stop playing."

"I'm not, I'm done! So, you might want to get to your wing before someone catches you with that."

He looked down at the brown paper sack and said, "You'll be back."

\*\*\*

### Hotboy

"Incoming!" the key boss yelled, announcing that I was coming on the wing. I walked past the officers' closet without looking to see which C.O. was working the wing. Whoever it was, I didn't want the person to stop me and try to search me. I walked the dayroom; it was completely empty.

"Gianni!" Grain shouted my name, stopping me in my tracks. "Damn, foreal! No *hey, how you doing*? Nothing!" I faced her and smiled. She had some clear lip gloss on that made her lips look super juicy.

"I didn't know you were here," I said. She walked away and went back to whatever she was doing in the officers' closet.

"Whatever! You know you saw me," she said.

I walked behind her. "I didn't see yo' short ass—Next time, stand on yo' tippy toes, I'll probably be able to see you then," I teased.

"I was—boy!" she punched me in my arm. She was sensitive when it came to her height. She told me once before, that she tried to go to the military, but she was too short. Since then, she took up the job as a C.O., in hopes of one day becoming a police officer.

I grabbed my arm, making it seem like she actually hit me hard. She looked at me and laughed. "Boy! You know that didn't hurt."

"Where is everyone? Why are we racked up?" I asked, looking at the empty dayroom.

"Because the warden said so. He said he didn't want what happened in the north chow hall to escalate to the south side, so he had us rack everyone up for the night."

"Oh yea', that means it's just you and me for the night. Bet that, let me go put this up, and I'll be right back."

She grabbed my arm and said, "Wait! What's that?" She reached for the johnny sack.

"It ain't none of yo' business."

She poked her lips out like a baby. "Please—let me see."

I was a gangsta at heart, but I was a straight sucka for a sexy ass woman. "Here." I handed her the sack.

She bounced up and down like she had won a prize. "What—what the hell is this?" she asked, while looking inside the bag. I snatched it back from her. "It ain't none of yo' business, like I told you. I'ma put this up, and I'll be right back." I ran off before she could argue.

Instead of going up the stairs, like I planned on doing, I walked down one row, to Eastwood's cell. He was lying down, with his headphones on. I thumped him on the head, scaring the shit out of him. He rubbed his head and said, "Come on, bitch! That shit hurts!"

I laughed. "You made it out, I see," I said. "What about Los?"

Eastwood sat up on his bunk and said, "Los should be in his cell. We walked out the chow hall together. That bitch Childs, she tried to say I was fighting. I told her yea'! Fighting to breathe! Them motherfuckers damn near killed me with all that ho ass gas!"

I laughed, remembering how hard he was coughing.

"Bitch, that ain't funny!" Eastwood said. "I haven't stopped wheezing since."

He made me laugh harder. His celly, who was a fat Hispanic laughed too. Eastwood looked at his celly and said, "Oh, it's funny! Get yo' fat ass on yo' bunk before I slap the shit outta you!"

I started laughing hard as hell. His celly's smile faded as he climbed on his bunk and laid still. I shook my head. A grown ass man—afraid of another man.

"I need a favor, my nigga," I said, kneeling down so that his celly couldn't hear.

"What's popping?" Eastwood said.

I pulled the drop out of the johnny sack, just a little, so that he could see. "I need you to hold this down for me 'til I go in the cell. Babe working over here, I'm tryna get som' pussy before the night is over with."

As soon as I said her name, Grain walked out of the officers' closet and flicked me off. Just for that, I was gon' punish her pussy.

Eastwood caught me in a trance. "You in love with that lil' bitch, ain't you?"

I shook my head and said, "I wouldn't call it love. I do cut for the lil' bitch, though. She cool peoples. She don't act funny with me, like she do other people. She's really laid back. But, you know, when a bitch get a taste of the dick master, her whole world changes." I laughed.

Eastwood held his chest as he laughed. "Dick master! Bitch ass nigga, get away from my cell with that shit!"

"Fo' real though, hold this down, and I gotcha." I handed the pack to him.

"Be careful," Eastwood said. "You know you ain't got nobody out there with you to watch out for you." Eastwood brought it to my attention.

"You know I got me," I said. "Them ho's couldn't catch me, if I gave 'em a head start."

\*\*\*

**Lt. McFee**

# Kingpen

"Lieu', can I have a word with you?" Officer Kiles asked.

I was just about to go on my lunch break. I needed a cigarette badly. My mind has been heavy since Thompson gave me the instructions—to help Gianni flood the unit with dope. I was contemplating not doing it. I knew if I didn't, somehow or some way, Thompson would find a way to do it, and get rid of me at the same time. I had worked too hard to just give my position up to someone that didn't deserve it. If all I had to do was, push a little dope, then that's what I'm going to do. *Damn*, I thought. *Am I a hypocrite?*

"What do you need?" I answered Kiles.

Kiles had been on my list for a few weeks now. I had a feeling that he was one of the officers that was bringing drugs to the unit.

"Sir, I just witnessed an inmate picking up a package that I suspect was drugs," Kiles said.

I looked at him. Maybe I misjudged him. "Who? Where?" I asked, ready to take the inmate down. I was caught in between being the best C.O. the penitentiary has ever seen and doing whatever it took to get a promotion.

"It was an inmate on H-wing. Inmate Kingsley. I don't know if you know him," Kiles said, as he went on to describe him.

Kingsley! Every time I heard his name, I got chills. Why was he always in the mix of something! It was like destiny had joined us at the hip. I couldn't dodge him. "Where is he now?" I asked.

"He's on his wing," Kiles said.

Kiles kept talking, but I ignored him and thought about how I was going to play everything. I patted Kiles on his shoulder and said, "Good job, son. I'll take it from here."

"Sir, I was thinking that I could maybe—come with you, to help you take him down." Kiles looked eager to help.

"Son, listen to me. Knowing Kingsley, he's probably got rid of the drop already. By the time we get to his wing, it'll be put up, and we will never be able to find it."

Kiles nodded and said, "So, what do we do?"

I laughed. "We don't do anything. You should go back to doing your job. I'll take it from here."

Kiles looked disappointed. I guess the rumors were wrong. Maybe he was a good C.O., unlike me. Kiles nodded and walked away. He seemed heart-broken. I walked in the Major's office. I logged on to an available computer and went to the cameras. I switched over to H-wing's cameras. I went back twenty minutes on the camera, so that I could watch Kingsley's every move. The camera showed Kingsley coming on the wing. He talked to the C.O. for a short minute, then he walked off. The camera showed him with a brown paper sack. He walked to another inmate's cell, and talked for a minute, before giving the inmate in the cell the brown sack. *Bingo!* I thought.

I went back to the live feed. The camera showed Kingsley in front of the officers' closet talking to the C.O. The door to the closet was swung open, so that the camera couldn't see past the door. Fuck! I thought. Blind spot! Kinglsey stepped in the closet and disappeared from the view of the camera.

\*\*\*

### Hotboy

"What you doing!"

I caught Grain off guard. She jumped, covering her mouth. "Boy! Don't scare me like that! That shit ain't funny!" she said, as I tried to hold my laugh in. She looked like she was really serious.

"My bad, babe. I didn't think you'll piss yo' pants." I

tried to lighten the mood.

She sat on the cooler in the officers' closet. Her legs were wide open, her camel toe was poking. I couldn't help but lick my lips. Her lil' ass had some sweet pussy. I wondered if she knew. Probably not, that's probably why she was still working here.

"So, are you going to tell me what you had wrapped in that duct tape? Or, am I going to have to call for rank?" she said with a smile,

I walked in the closet and grabbed her by the neck. I applied a little pressure, just enough to make her gasp. "You wouldn't do yo' man like that. Would you?" I asked.

She moaned as I leaned in and kissed her on the lips, then I softly bit her on the lip. "Ouch! Bastard!" She shoved. I laughed. I did bite her pretty hard. "Who says you're my man, anyway? When did we make that official?" she asked.

I pinched her nose. For some reason, I liked touching her skin. "The day you said you love me," I free-styled.

She cocked her head to the side and said, "I never said that!"

"Yeah, you did. When you had my dick in yo' mouth, you said, *mm—mmm—mmmm!*" I laughed.

She jumped up and punched me. "Jerk! I swear, I can't stand yo' black ass!" she said, as she sat down on the cooler. "Well, you said the same thing when you were lapping my juices up. You said, *Mhhmm—mhhhh!*" She made loud slurping noises.

I fell over, laughing. She was something else. "Okay, that's fair—It did taste good, though," I said.

Her laugh subsided; her face expression became filled with lust. She tried to change the subject. "So, what was in that black tape?" she asked.

"A bomb," I answered. We used the term bomb, because if you were to get caught with it, you'll die. By dying, we meant a penitentiary death. You'll get shipped to another unit, and no one would ever see you again.

"Where did you get it?" she asked. I wasn't up for a game of twenty-one questions

"I got it from a C.O. This chick be helping me out every now and then."

She sat upright and mugged me. "What the fuck you mean, a female C.O.? What do you give her in return?" She was in her feelings, exactly where I needed her to be.

"What the fuck you mean, what do I give her in return!" I spat. "Whatever she asks for. Money, dick, protection."

"Dick!" she said, like everything else didn't matter. "Ugh! I know you ain't fucking other bitches in here, unprotected!" she said, her veins showing on her forehead.

It took everything in me not to laugh. I knew how to bring the emotions out of a bitch. "Other bitches! So that's what you call yo'self?"

She sighed. "You know what I meant. Don't play with me right now! You mean to tell me, this whole time you've been messing with me, you've been fucking another bitch, too. I knew it! You were too good to be true!" She shook her head.

"Chill the fuck out! I met her before you even started working here. I haven't dealt with the bitch in over three months."

"Well, why in the hell is she bringing you whatever the fuck that is she's bringing you?" she asked.

I laid the cake batter, whipped it up, and let the bitch bake until it was fluffy. Now all I had to do was, apply the icing. "'Cause, the bitch want som' dick, and I'm broke! What else do you expect me to do? Huh?"

She waved her hand and shook her head at me. "Unuhh! Tell whoever the bitch is, *no* can do! Tell her, mama got it! Her services are no longer needed. She can pay another nigga for some dick, but it damn sure won't be yours!" she said.

Damn, I was good! "What the fuck you mean, tell her

naw? Didn't you hear me say, *I'm broke*. I need whatever a bitch is willing to give me. I ain't tryna come home broke!" I said, laying it on thick.

"Like I said, tell her—her services are no longer needed. Whatever you need, money, food, I'll bring it to you. Ain't no mo' dick selling going on over here." She stood up, her lil' ass was only tall enough to reach my chest.

"Ma, you talking like you really about that life— You ain't ready for no shit like that," I said, reeling her in.

She grabbed my dick through my pants and squeezed it. "I know one thing. You better not give *this* to anyone else!" She applied pressure.

"Come on, girl! That shit hurts!" I whined.

"It'll be worse if I find out you giving my shit away again. You think I'm playing, fucking try me again!" She gave it one last squeeze before letting go. I grabbed her by her neck again. I forced my weight on her, forcing her to sit on the cooler. "You don't run shit! I run this, you hear me? What I say, goes!" I slightly shoved her by the throat.

She looked up at me with lust-filled eyes. Reaching for my waistband, she freed my dick. My one-eyed monster woke up as soon as he felt her touch. She stared into my eyes as she kissed the head. "You—Better—Not—Give— This—To—Anyone—Else!" She punctuated each of those words with a kiss to emphasize her point.

Her soft kisses had me rock-hard. I didn't know that my eyes were closed, until she stopped. "Ma, stop playing! If this yo' dick, then own this big mo'fucka!" I said.

She bit the head with the tip of her teeth. That shit sent chills down my spine. She dragged her teeth all the way down to the base. I started shaking like a stripper. It felt so good, my knees started to buck. She stopped teasing and let me feel the warmth of her mouth.

"That's it, babe! Take control!" I said, as she bobbed her head up and down. She stroked the base every time her lips came to the tip. She was a professional dick sucker. In my book, she was the G.O.A.T.

"Auhhh!" she came up for air. Spit came from her mouth. She swiped it with her tongue and smiled.

"Damn, girl! I love that freaky shit," I said.

She laughed and stood up. "I know you do. I also know you love this, too!" She unbuttoned, then unzipped her pants, and they fell to the floor. She faced the cooler, her ass facing me. She hooked her thong with her finger, and slid it to the side. I squatted down and buried my face between her ass cheeks. She smelled like strawberries.

"Ahh! Fuck! She panted, as she placed her hand on the wall for balance. My tongue was digging in her like a gynecologist. She always brought that freaky shit out of me. Every time I saw her, I just wanted to taste her. Tonight though, I didn't just want to taste her. Tonight, I was gon' get full. Her lil' ass started twerking on my tongue. I knew I was doing my best shit!

"Fuck, bae! Eat my ass, babe! Ohh—shiit! It feels *so* good!" she moaned so loud, I almost got scared and stopped.

"Shit!" she moaned, as I spread her cheeks wider, sticking my tongue down to the bottom of her asshole. Her hand fell down to her side, and she began to shiver. I knew she was on the verge of cumming.

"No, you don't! —" I stopped before she could cum. She gasped and looked back.

"What? Why you stop?" she asked, her legs barely holding her up.

"I told you, I run this! You don't cum until I tell you to cum! Now, face the shelf!" I demanded.

Lust filled her eyes. She looked possessed. She faced the shelf.

"Put your leg on the bottom shelf." I stood behind her. I stroked my dick and aimed the head at her entrance. I eased inside her tight hole. I could feel her tight walls brushing against the veins on my dick.

"Sssss!" she moaned as her walls clamped around my member. I had to stroke upwards, instead of straight, because my dick curved like a banana. With her being so short, and us being in a tight space, it started off complicated. After a few strokes, I mastered it, and she was screaming my name in bliss.

"Gianni! Daddee! —It feels *so* good!—It fits perfectly," she moaned.

I was tossing that lil' pussy all over the place. "This what you want? Huh?" I said, more of a statement.

"Yes! Give it to me! Please! Ohh, fuck! Yess!" she moaned, as I gripped her ass, leaving my handprint.

"You gon' follow my lead?" I asked, as I long stroked her pussy.

"Ahh, yes! Whatever—whatever you want, daddy! Just—fuck me!" she begged.

I pulled out, leaned over, and bit her on her ass. I slipped back in and did what I do best. I wanted her to remember this. 'Cause the next time, it'll cost her!

## Chapter Eighteen

### Gabby

"Come on, Gabby," I said to myself. "Just a little—further!" I tried my hardest to reach my fanny pack, to retrieve my phone. My forehead was covered with sweat. My leg had begun to bleed again from the constant moving. It smelled awful. Like it was infected. I was in so much pain. But I'd rather feel pain than to not be able to feel at all. Within a few hours, I made it halfway to the stairs. I had to keep taking frequent breaks to prevent myself from vomiting. I had never felt so much pain in all of my life. My leg would go completely numb, scaring the crap out of me. Then the feeling would come back, with the worse pain I've ever felt.

The basement door opened, stopping me in my tracks. Once the light came on, I saw that it wasn't Seth, but Kelly, walking down the stairs. She had some of my clothes on that fitted her perfectly. She even had my hair pin in her hair.

"Hey, Gabby, I—uh brought you something to eat," she said, holding a plate with a sandwich in her left hand and a Gatorade in her right hand.

I looked at her, amazed. She had fixed herself up, and she actually looked pretty, too. Just not prettier than me. I sat upright, being careful not to let her see what I was trying to do.

Kelly stepped closer with the plate and said, "I thought you might've been hungry. You've been down here for a week now. I can only imagine what you're going through." She sat the food in front of me. Kelly looked at me with such pity. Like I was the one who's the dope fiend, and she was the saint. Then she had the nerve to say, she could only imagine. I swear, if I could stand up! I'd put my hair in a bun and beat her out of everything she had on that's mine. "You can only imagine!" I said sarcastically. "Kelly, really! No, you can't imagine, because it's not you that's down here dying!" I shouted. "You're upstairs! In my bed! Sleeping with my fiancé! Pshh!" I smacked my lips. "You can only imagine!" I said, more to myself. I was heated. Not only was I bleeding to death. But I was kidnapped in my own damn house. And this—bitch! Ughh—this bitch!

"I deserved that; I do." Kelly held her hands up. "I swear, I didn't put Seth up to this." She took a seat on the couch. "He found me!" She started crying. "He found me—inside a dope house." She wiped the tears from her cheek and said, "Seth found me—after—after I'd been raped." She sighed and said, "I was raped by my dealer. Seth killed him for me. I didn't ask for him to. I didn't even know that he was there." She wiped her eyes, and nervously played with her fingers. "I had been clean for months. Until I came here one day. I knocked on the door, and Seth answered. Then Jacob—"

She smiled as she said his name. "Jacob ran behind him. My little boy—"

She sobbed again. "My little boy didn't even know who I was. His own mother! That crushed me. I felt lower than the dirt on the ground." She wiped her face and took a moment to gather herself. "Seth denied me the opportunity to see Jacob. So, I went to the dope house to get high. It was the only way that I could numb the pain. I asked my dealer for the best dope that he had. He had to have put something in my batch, because I passed out. Next thing I know, I woke up in my underwear, in Seth's arms." I couldn't believe this bitch! She had the nerve to tell me her sob story. Like I gave a fuck. She wanted me to have sympathy for her, when I was the one sitting on the ground, bleeding out. I honestly hated the fact that she got raped, but that was her own fault. I would never experience her pain, because I would never be caught in a dope house. "I'm sorry to hear that, Kelly. I know it must be hard for you." I played the sympathy role. One thing about us women—We came closer together when we cried together. "I had been telling Seth for years to let you see Jacob. He would always say, she ain't clean, you're his mom, now." I lied, pulling all the tricks out the hat.

She looked down at me, her eyes full of disappointment. "Did he really say that?" she asked.

I nodded.

"He told me, it was always you telling him not to let me see Jacob."

I shook my head and said, "No, girl! I would never keep a woman from her child."

She sighed and said: "Every day, I thought about Jacob. Every night, when I was getting high, I prayed for him. Last night, he looked at me when I walked in his room. He said, 'Miss, I want my mommy. My daddy hurt my mommy'."

I looked at her as she broke down. I actually felt sorry for her now. I knew what it felt like to actually lose a child. The heartache of having those *what-if* thoughts. I would always think about Gianni Jr. *What kind of mom would I have been to him? What kind of father Gianni would've been to his son!* Thinking about everything, I started crying. "You know, I just lost a baby," I said. "A boy—*Gianni, Jr.*, would've been his name."

Kelly looked at me with a confused look. "Gianni, Jr.?"

I sighed as a laugh managed to escape. Yea'— Gianni, Junior. I—uh—I met his father when I was working in TDC. We met on the Beto unit." I smiled, thinking about everything. "I actually didn't plan on anything transpiring between us. I just wanted to do my job, take care of my family, and go home every day." I laughed and said, "Funny how life works. I actually fell in love with Gianni. As I look at all of this mess, I actually deserve it."

Kelly scooted off the couch and sat beside me on the floor. She looked at me first, then she pulled me in for a hug. "Gabby, I'm so, sorry. I didn't know." She looked at me and said. "Do you think that's why Seth is acting the way he's acting?"

I nodded. "That—and you."

The way we looked sitting beside each other on the floor, you would think we were best friends.

"I didn't mean for any of this to happen," Kelly said. "When I first met Seth, he wasn't like this. I mean, yeah, he had some things he struggled with, like trust. But he wasn't like, this." She used the couch to help herself up. "I think I can help you get out of here." She walked off.

"How are you going to help me, and you're leaving me?" She stopped at the first step and looked back. "I'm going to do him like I used to do him, when I wanted something from him." She smiled. "Seth, could never deny *Miss Marvelous*," she said as she patted her pussy. "I got the best pussy he's ever had."

I shook my head. "No! What are you talking about? All you have to do is, help me up, and I'll leave. Please!"

She looked confused, "I can't! Seth would kill me if he found out I helped you."

Kelly had me fooled. She was talking like she was going to help me. This whole time, she's been forming a plan to seduce Seth. "Kelly, you don't understand. I'm dying down here. You have to help me before he gets home. Please!"

"So he can kill me, too. Seth's upstairs lying down. I can't, Gabby. I'm sorry. Please, just let me do this my way. Watch, it'll work." Kelly walked up the stairs, cutting the light off behind her. She didn't have the decency to even leave the light on for me.

I couldn't believe her stupid ass tactic. All she had to do was, help me up the stairs, and I would be free. As dumb as she was, I felt sorry for Jacob. He had two dumbass parents.

Minutes later, cement crumbs fell from the ceiling. The

floor above me began to squeak. I knew that sound from anywhere. The sounds of love making.

\*\*\*

### Seth

"Oh, fuck! Arhh, damn babe! It's been a long time!" Kelly moaned, as she rode me like she'd never done before. And it felt amazing. Her ass was bigger and softer than I could remember. Even her titties were bigger.

We started the night off by getting as high as we could get. She cooked me a fast meal. Fish, with some white rice. Me, Kelly, and Jacob ate as a family for the first time. The food was good. Jacob barely touched his food. I could tell he was still upset about Gabby. I had called Jacob in the kitchen after dinner for some ice cream. He looked at the basement door. Then he ran to his room, crying. He had to get that side of him from his mother. He damn sure didn't get that shit from me. I blame Gabby, really. At times, Jacob could be so soft. I told Gabby to stop calling him a damn teapot. They hear that shit and go soft.

"Babe, are you okay?"

Kelly snapped me back to reality. My hand was around her throat. Her face was red, a tear escaped her eye. I was so deep in thought that I didn't know that I was choking her. I stopped midstroke and caressed her cheek. "I'm sorry, babe—I can't do this," I said, as I pulled out and sat on the edge of the bed. "I have so much running through my mind at the moment." I looked at her neck. My handprints were imprinted in her neck. "I could've choked you out."

Kelly crawled over to me and said, "It's okay, Seth. I understand what you're going through. Look, this whole thing, today—the dinner, the sex—I planned it all."

My dick instantly went limp. "What you mean, you planned this?" I asked.

She stood up and walked over to me. Her naked body smelled of sweat. "I went down to the basement earlier," she said, as I looked at her like she disobeyed me. "I know, I know." She raised her hand up before I could curse her the fuck out. "I took her some food and something to drink." She continued, "I felt sorry for her, Seth. We talked, and I—told her I would talk to you about letting her go."

I couldn't believe she went behind my back and did anything for Gabby. I blame myself for leaving the lock off the damn door. "So, this—" I pointed to her naked body. "This was all just to lure me in, so you could convince me to let her go?"

Kelly squeezed my hands and said, "That was until right now. When we ate dinner, I changed my mind. If you were to let her go, there's no way she won't call the police. I can't take the chance of me losing you again." She kissed my hand and brought it to her cheek.

I pulled her close to me, her titties just inches from my lips. "So, what makes me think you're not still trying to lure me in?" I asked.

She kissed my forehead, my nose, and then my lips. "Feeling you inside me made me realize that you've been giving her what belongs to me. How this bed is where y'all made love! How my son, our son, don't even know I'm his mom. Seth, when you rescued me that night, did you know that he raped me?"

Her eyes began to water. I kissed her hands. The left one, then the right one. "No, babe. I didn't know. I assumed he planned on it, but I didn't know he actually did. I saw your jeans, the same ones you wore over here that night. That's how I knew you were there. I'm sorry! I—I wish I could've gotten there faster." I was now in tears. Using meth always made me an emotional person.

We cried together as she kissed my lips.

"Thank you for what you did—The way you rode for me, I have to ride for you the same way," she said.

I pulled her naked body in my lap, she straddled me. I slipped inside her wetness. She rode me as tears fell down her cheeks. "Uhh!" she moaned, as I pulled her body down, filling her up.

Right when I got back in the groove, the damn doorbell rang. Kelly leaned in to kiss me. I dodged her kiss, focusing my attention on the doorbell. She kept riding me, like I was the last piece of dick on earth. She kissed my neck and moaned loud.

"Shhh! Hol' up," I whispered. I was so high I didn't know I was whispering in my own damn house. The doorbell rang two more times. This time, the person at the door was more urgent. I stood up. Kelly wrapped her legs around my waist. She was so caught up in getting her nut; she didn't care that someone was at the door.

"Bae, hol' up. Someone's at the door."

She ignored me as she bounced up and down on my dick. "So! Ohh, uhhh! Forget—them!" she moaned.

She continued to bounce on me like a pogo stick. If the doorbell wouldn't have rang, I would've been all into it, but I remembered Gabby was downstairs in the basement. Knowing what she did when Lakewood dropped by, she would probably try it again.

"It could be anyone," I said, as the doorbell turned into heavy knocks. "It could be the police. Do you hear how they're knocking?" I tossed her little ass on the bed. Her cum slid down my leg as I ran to the bathroom to grab my robe. I ran to the kitchen to make sure the basement door was still locked. Running back to the restroom, I grabbed my gun, and hid it in the nightstand by the bed. As I closed the drawer, heavy knocks dug into the front door.

"I'm coming!" I yelled. "Give me a second!"

Peeping through the peephole, I damn near shitted on myself.

"Who is it?" Kelly whispered from behind me.

I smacked the side of my head with the palm of my

hand.

"What, bae? Who is it?" Kelly asked, seeing my reaction.

The loud knocks came again, startling us. "Mr. Kiles, if you're in there, it's important that you open up!" a police officer shouted through the door.

Kelly looked worried. I guess all that bullshit she was talking about riding went out the window. Kelly fled to the bedroom, went to the bathroom, and closed the door behind her. I wiped my face and looked myself over before I opened the door. "How may I help you, officer?" I asked, as I faked a yawn.

A bald, Caucasian officer—with a mask on—stood on the other side of the door. His name tag read: Smith. He was alone, which was good. "Are you Mr. Kiles?" Officer Smith asked.

Nodding, I said, "That's me! Can I ask, what's this all about?"

"We received a missing person's report by a woman who claims her daughter, a Ms. Gabriela Newton, stays here." He read from his notepad.

"Missing!" I said with a laugh. "I wouldn't say, missing."

"Do you know of her whereabouts?" he asked.

I looked over my shoulder and said, "Yea', she's in the bathroom right now."

Officer Smith looked over my shoulder and said, "Do you mind if I talk to her? That way, we can close this case."

"Sure! Step in, and I'll go get her." I walked off, leaving the door open. Officer Smith stepped in and closed the door behind him.

"Gabby, babe!" I yelled towards the bathroom. I opened the bathroom door to find Kelly sitting on the toilet, smoking a cigarette. I leaned into her ear and whispered, "I need for you to pretend to be Gabby. He came looking for her. So, if he thinks that you're her, he'll leave.

She shook her head and said, "I don't look anything like her. No! That's insane!" She took another pull from the cigarette.

"Kelly, I need you! You just said, you were riding with me, so come on!" I reminded her.

She huffed, then stood up. Grabbing Gabby's robe, she said, "How old is she? I'll need her birthdate, and her middle name."

I smiled and said, "Gabriela Skylar Newton. June 25th, 1995." I kissed her as we walked out the bathroom together.

"Hi, officer!—I'm sorry to keep you waiting," Kelly said, extending her hand, and Officer Smith shook it.

"Is it okay—if I may?" Officer Smith asked, gesturing to the couch.

"Oh, yes!" She laughed. "I'm sorry, where are my manners, please do." Kelly played host. Kelly sat on the edge of the couch, facing the officer, while I sat in the lazy boy chair. Officer Smith took out his notepad and flipped it to a specific section. "I'm sorry to bother you so late, Ms.—" he said.

"Newton!" Kelly finished his sentence.

"Yes, Newton. I—uh—I talked to your mother. She reported you missing. She claimed she hadn't heard from you in a week. She said that you and her made sure to talk to each other at least three times a week. She said she's worried about you, that you would've called by now." He looked up at her and said, "She also said that you're in a wheelchair."

Kelly smiled and said, "I can't call her because I can't find my phone. I think my son might've misplaced it. I recently came from therapy. I couldn't walk as good. But I'm fine now. I've been so busy, trying to get everything in order for this coronavirus crap, it must've slipped my mind to call her and tell her I was okay." She said it like she had done this before.

Officer Smith raised his hand and smiled. "It's fine, I

understand. A worried parent is a good parent. But by protocol, I have to ask you a few questions." He laughed. "You know, make sure you are who you say you are."

Kelly laughed like she thought that shit was funny. "Seriously! Do people pretend to be someone else in situations like this?" Kelly asked.

"You have no idea." He laughed. "So—your middle name?" Officer Smith asked

"Skylar!" Kelly responded quick.

"Date of birth?" he asked.

"June twenty-fifth, nineteen ninety-five," she answered.

Officer Smith stood up as he closed his notepad. "Again, I'm sorry about this," he said. "People don't hear from their loved ones, and they think the worse. But it's good to have people that care enough about you that will call us when they fear the worse. So, consider yourself lucky, and whenever you get a chance, call your mom, she's worried sick about you." He laughed.

Seeing him off to the door, we joined in on a laugh. Opening the door, I said: "Don't worry, I'll drive her to see her tomorrow. Thank you, for following up also. There are still some good officers out there." I was ready to go back in the bedroom and finish what me and Kelly had started. I owed her the best dick she's ever had, for the amazing job she just did.

Officer Smith stood on the opposite side of the door and shook my hand. Before I could let go of his hand, a window shattered, and a screaming woman's voice echoed throughout the quiet night.

"Help! I'm down here!"

## Chapter 18

### Hotboy

"Damn, babe! —That was sweet," Grain said, as she zipped up her pants.

I wiped the sweat from my forehead with the bottom of my shirt. Babe had some bomb ass pussy. Every time I got with her, it was like my first time all over again. "You ain't lying, it was alright," I said.

She shoved me. "Alright! Boy, stop! You was moaning louder than me."

"It was good, ma. But can you top it?" I asked, as I gripped her ass, pulling her close to me for a kiss.

"Mhhh! Of course, I can, but can you?" she countered.

"Trust me, you ain't seen shit yet," I said, as I lifted her off the ground by her ass. She wrapped her legs around my waist.

Her walkie-talkie went off, saying that it was time for count. "You got lucky!" I said, as I let her go.

She grabbed her count sheets and clipboard. "Don't worry, it's still early—We have all night," she said, as she brushed her ass against my dick.

I watched her lil' ass, as she walked off to count. She was sexy without even knowing it. I dragged the cooler out the closet and sat it by the dayroom door against the wall. "Count time, one row!" I yelled, letting everyone know what was going on. I know if she was to catch someone doing something he didn't have any business doing, she wouldn't turn him in. But then you had the jackers; besides, I wasn't a cock blocker, and I was out here on the run. So, no matter if she was my bitch or not, I still had to let them get their rocks off. That's just how the game goes. Once a nigga gets his nut, he's going to sleep.

Mirrors came out their cell bars once everyone heard it

was count time. I turned my back, facing the main gate. The face that I saw was smiling at me. But wasn't shit funny!

\*\*\*

### Lt. McFee

I had seen enough. The camera had showed Kingsley giving a brown sack to another inmate. Then he went in the officers' closet, and stayed in there with the officer, for over twenty minutes. There was no doubt in my mind, they were having sex. I logged out and walked to H-wing. I stuck my hand in my pocket, as I felt the bottle of K2 spray that O.I.G Thompson gave me. I had a job to do. By any means necessary. I stopped in front of H-wing's gate. The key boss saw me and went for his keys to unlock the gate. I waved him off. I still wasn't ready yet. I wanted to try to catch them in the act. I've been dying to see Grain naked. I listened closely, awaiting a moan, or anything that could me tell that they were still partying. My walkie-talkie went off. It was count time. I peeped around the corner. I saw Grain brush against Kingsley as she went off to count.

I ducked behind the wall, as Kingsley dragged the cooler out of the officers' closet. I could only imagine what different positions he had her in on the cooler. Lucky bastard! I never understood how a woman could come to work in here, seeing how the inmates are treated, and still want them. For God's sake, they wear each other's boxers; they have to go to sleep when we tell them, and wake up when we tell them.

I peeped around the corner again. Kingsley was standing with his back to me. I smiled, as I watched him watch her. He turned around, his eyes widened once he saw me. I smiled at him. I looked at the key boss and motioned for him to open the gate. Kingsley looked over his shoulders and yelled that I was coming on the wing. I didn't care who he warned, I already knew where everything was. I stepped on the wing and took a deep breath. I wanted to let him know that I could still smell their sex in the air.

"Smells like—ahhh!" I sniffed again. "Smells like sex on the beach."

"What? You just got done fucking one of your male C.O.'s?" he asked, trying to be funny.

"Be careful, Kingsley. You don't have any room for jokes." I walked in the officers' closet and looked through Officer Grain's tote bag. All she had was some bubble gum, five dollars in singles, and some Doritos.

"You find what you're looking for?" Kingsley asked with a laugh.

"No, but I'm close," I said, walking in the direction of his friend's cell.

"One row crawling!" he yelled, as I walked down one row. "This is Lt. McFee, I need backup on H-wing." I spoke into the walkie-talkie. H-wing's front gate swung open, and four C.O.'s ran on the wing, ready for action. "Contain him." I pointed to Kingsley, as I walked in the direction of my destination.

***

**Eastwood**

"We come from poverty, man, we ain't have a thing—" I rapped along to my favorite song—'*Pop Out*'—playing on 97.9 F.M. The beat was jamming tonight. I had my headphones turned up to the max. I started mumbling on the parts that I didn't know, then the DJ switched to a different song. I didn't like the song that came on, so I turned my radio down.

"McFee crawling down the ace!" I could hear Hotboy's voice from a distance. I jumped up and grabbed my hand mirror. By the time I got the mirror out the bars, McFee was standing in front of my cell door. He looked at me and smiled. I looked up at my celly, who was sitting with his legs Indian-style, just staring at me. His fat, bitch ass knew Mc Fee was on the wing, and ain't try to tell me. I should have beat his bitch ass up when I had the chance.

I looked down at the brown paper sack that Hotboy had gave me to hold. I knew that I could flush whatever it was before McFee opened my cell door.

"Don't even think about it!" McFee said, as if he was reading my thoughts.

"The water is off, so—just hand it over, I know it's in there," he said.

I grabbed the pack off the floor and ran to the toilet. I pushed the toilet button, and nothing happened. I tried again, nothing.

"Fuck!" I cursed. I was trapped, with no way of escaping.

Two more officers walked behind McFee to help him. "Just face the toilet, and make this easy on yourself," McFee instructed.

I dropped the pack on the floor and fell down to my knees. I cursed as I put my hands behind my head. I got caught slipping. But how? How did he know I had anything in here?

The door rolled as I awaited the cold steel cuffs that I had become accustomed to. McFee slapped his cuffs on me, then he bent down to grab the pack off the floor. "Take him to X-wing," he said. "I still have to thank his homie, Hotboy," McFee said, throwing me for a loop.

***

### Hotboy

"Fuck!" I cursed, as I watched two C.O.'s escort Eastwood out his cell in cuffs. McFee walked close behind with a brown johnny sack. The brown johnny sack that I gave to Eastwood to hold. Had McFee been watching me? He couldn't have, or else he would've caught me and Grain.

"Kingsley, I want to thank you," McFee said, as him, two C.O.'s, along with Eastwood, stood in front of me. Eastwood looked at me like I had betrayed him.

"Is this play sour?" Eastwood asked me in code, if I set him up.

"You know me better than that," I assured him.

Eastwood stared at me. I knew that look: the look of doubt. From the outside looking in, I looked like I did some foul shit. I couldn't win for losing.

Grain walked down the stairs as she added up her count. McFee smiled, as she walked closer to us.

"What happened?" she asked McFee.

"Nothing. I have it all under control," Mc.Fee said, looking from me to her. "Follow me, Kingsley," he said.

I looked behind me. Every inmate had their mirrors out their cells looking at us. "I'm not going anywhere without you putting me in cuffs—I already see what you trying to do," I said.

"Cuff him and bring him to my office."

\*\*\*

"Have a seat!" McFee said. He went behind his desk and logged on to his computer. "I see you've been really busy lately," he said, looking to me.

"I don't know what you're talking about," I said, nonchalant.

"Oh, you dont?" he said, as he typed something on his computer. He turned the computer screen to me and pressed play. The videos was of me leaving to go to the shower, and a short while later, Eastwood did the same.

"So what! You got me on camera going to the shower, what does that supposed to mean?" I asked, not seeing the purpose for the video.

"Look at the date, smart ass!" he said. I looked at the bottom of the video, and saw the date, but nothing registered to me. "That date doesn't ring a bell?" he asked. "How about two dead inmates in the shower? Does that ring a bell?" he said, then laughed.

Everything came back to me. That was the same night we killed Dame, and his homie. "My nigga, don't waste my time, what the fuck do you want from me?"

"As of right now, I don't want nothing from you, but you will want something from me." He stood up and walked around his desk. "See, right now, your homie is sitting in a holding cell, freezing his ass off, thinking about how you set him up."

"Fuck you mean? I ain't set nobody up!" I spat."

Only you and I know that, but what will your people think? Hotboy—if I may call you that—I heard that your name isn't as golden as it used to be." He was fucking with me. "I heard you're one foot in, and one foot out," he added.

"You went over my head a long time ago. I'm lost, and I ain't tryna be found, so if you ain't about to lock me up, can I go back to my wing, so that I won't get caught in count?"

"How about I dumb it down for you then? Your homie, he's about to go down for all that dope we found in his cell, and he's going to go down for two murders. You're going down for two murders, and this time, you're not getting away with it, we have your footprints, and footage of both of you leaving the wing ten minutes before the bodies were found in the shower. So, do I have your attention now?"

I didn't want to say too much, because he got off on seeing niggas sweat. "What do you want? I ain't no snitch, so try something else. If you had anything on me, why haven't my rights been read to me? I think you bluffing." I knew the deck was stacked against me, but he only knew what he had in his hand; he didn't know what cards I held.

"I tell you what. Don't do what I want, and you'll see if I'm bluffing."

"What is it that you want?" I asked. I knew it was probably some snitch shit that I wasn't about to get involved in. Whatever he had planned, it wasn't going to be good. Doing a deal with him, was worse than doing a deal with the devil.

Lt. McFee went on telling me what he wanted me to do, in exchange for Eastwood's alibi for the two bodies that were found in the shower. I never admitted to the murders, but I did accept his offer. "No consequences, at all?" I asked for assurance.

"None! But remember our deal, you didn't get this from me," he said.

I smiled and said, "Hear no evil, speak no evil!"

# Kingpen

## Chapter 19

### Newton

My stomach growled for the umpteenth time. The sandwich did little to my appetite. I held my stomach as I turned to the sound of a car pulling up in the driveway. The headlights flashed through the small basement window before the engine shut off. It had to be a visitor, because I didn't hear Seth or Kelly leave. Maybe it was Lakewood again, coming to deliver more drugs. That thought crossed my mind, until I heard the doorbell ring. A drug dealer never rang the doorbell. They always called or texted to let you know they were outside. I tried to be still as possible to see if I could hear a voice, or a specific sound. Hearing nothing in particular, I waited in silence. The doorbell rang again, this time more urgent than before. Then came the heavy knocks. Only two people ever beat on the door that way. A mistress—and the police. As bad as I wanted to scream for help, I couldn't, because I didn't know exactly where Seth was. I didn't want to upset him so that he could hit me with his gun again. That shit hurt like hell.

The heavy knocks started again. A loud voice came over the knocks. It was the police. "Mr. Kiles, if you're in there, it's important that you open up." I wondered what made them finally come. Did Lakewood hear me, and alert the police? Or maybe my mom started to worry about me. I wanted to scream for help. But, seeing that the police was outside, and Seth was inside, I had a greater chance of getting killed, than the chance of getting rescued. I could barely hear what Seth said, as he answered the door. Their conversation grew faint as my stomach growled the rest of their conversation out.

"If you be quiet, maybe I can get us out of here," I said to my stomach.

I heard footsteps above my head, small ones. I prayed:

"Lord, please! Please help me get out of here. I beg for your mercy, don't let me die down here. Not like this." A thought came to my mind—how I had hit the window when Lakewood was here. If I would've had something heavier, I would've got his attention. I looked to my fanny pack. I had no other choice. It was either get to my phone or die. I lifted my head to God, asking him for his strength. I painfully crawled over to my fanny pack. I sighed as my hands touched it. I took a deep breath as I unzipped it.

I pulled my phone out, and what I saw knocked the wind out of me. The screen was shattered. As I held on to the power button, the phone lit up, then it turned back off. The fucking battery was dead. I let out a waterfall of tears. I looked at the phone in my hand, then to the window. "Thank you, God," I said to myself. If I could hit the window with the phone, I'm sure it'll crack the glass; if not, break it. I had to hit it right on the money.

Seeing that Kelly didn't come back, I guess her pussy wasn't as good as she thought. Now I had to take matters into my own hands.

I clutched the phone as I did a little practice throw. I remembered how the quarterbacks would move their arm back and forth over their heads before the game. I did a few of those until my arm loosened up. I heard the front door open, along with Seth's voice. He was lying to the police about taking me to see my mother. I felt betrayed by a man that I shouldn't have loved. The anger and betrayal boiled up on the inside of me. Kelly, with her fake tears—If she was in front of me, I would've strangled her to death. I thought we had a girls' moment, shiesty bitch! I threw the phone at the window, imagining that the window was her face. The phone went straight through the window, shattering the glass.

Once I realized what I did, I screamed.

\*\*\*

# Concrete Killa 2

## Seth

"Help! I'm down here!" Gabby screamed.

First, I heard the shattered glass, then her cries. The sound of her cries were deafening through the quiet night. All three of us were stuck in a trance. I didn't know how to react. Kelly was even in another world. Officer Smith reached for his gun. He knew exactly where the pleas were coming from.

"Help me, officer! I'm down here!" Gabby yelled again.

Officer Smith pulled his gun and aimed it at us. "Step back! Who was that?" he asked, as he took a step towards us. Kelly held her hands up and cried. The bitch was a dead giveaway

"Where is she? Was that Newton?" he asked, yelling.

I ignored his questions as I took a step backwards. We were already busted, there was no point in snitching on myself. You could hear Gabby screaming louder and louder. She was screaming her name, and how she had been kidnapped, and that she was in the basement, and she couldn't walk.

Officer Smith nudged his gun at me and said, "Take me to her!"

I held my hands up and said, "Okay, take it easy. She's downstairs, in the basement." I pointed in the direction of the basement. "Whatever you do, please don't shoot. My son is in the other room."

"Screw you! You sick bastard! And you too!" he said to Kelly. "Pretending to be someone else, you people are sick! You don't deserve a son."

"Look, I'm going to take you to her, but I have to turn my back to you—Don't shoot me," I said.

He gripped his gun tighter, aiming it at my back. "Don't try anything," he said to me. "And—you, stay where I can see you," he said to Kelly.

Kelly looked pale in the face. I knew the drugs were causing it. Me, on the other hand, I was pumped up. I felt like superman. I figured I could wrestle him down, and take his gun from him, but that may alarm the neighbors. I thought about doing the move from *Rush Hour*, when Jackie Chan took the gun from Chris Tucker, but I figured he was trained for stuff like that.

I kept my head forward, as I escorted him to the kitchen. The key was still inside the lock; the lock was hanging from the hook on the door.

"Open it!" Officer Smith said, "And you, stand over there," he said to Kelly. Kelly followed his instructions and stood by the kitchen sink.

I lifted the lock and tossed it on the floor. I opened the door and looked back at the officer. "Turn the light on! Hurry up!" he said. Nervously, I looked at Kelly as she cried. I hate that I dragged her into this predicament. I had failed her yet again. I pulled the string, and the light to the basement came on. "Let's go! Move it!" Officer Smith ordered. He pointed his gun, with the intention to kill if I made one false move.

I walked down the steps slowly. As I walked down the steps, I was able to see Gabby. She looked horrible. Her hair was a mess. She was covered in dirt, and she smelled foul, like congealed blood.

"Oh! Thank God!" Gabby said, as she saw the officer behind me.

"Gabriela Newton?" he asked her.

She nodded as the tears fell. "Yes! Yes, I'm Gabriela Skylar Newton! Thank you so much!" she said as she crawled over to us.

"Don't move! I'll call for some help," he said, as he reached for his walkie-talkie. Dispatch! This is—"

"*Bak! Bak!*" the gun echoed loudly throughout the basement. The officer caught one slug to the neck, and the other to his vest. "*Bak!*" Officer Smith's gun went off in the air, as he fell clutching his neck. Blood splattered and seeped through his fingers.

"No!" Gabby screamed, as she crawled over to his body. Kelly dropped the smoking gun and covered her mouth with her shaking hands. Shaking her head, she said, "I didn't mean to—I was just trying—!" she cried.

"Babe, it's okay! Come here." I pulled her in for a hug. Snot, mixed with tears, ran down her face. "He's dying! We have to save him! I'll go to jail! They'll never let me out! We—have to!" Kelly cried, as she ran over to the officer's body. She kneeled down beside Gabby. Gabby's hand was over the officer's hand. You could hear the sound that everyone calls the death whistle. Officer Smith's last breath. It was loud, in that quiet moment.

Kelly looked back at me. I felt her pain. What she just did could get her a life sentence, or worse, the death penalty. Kidnapping Gabby was considered a felony but killing a cop—That was on a whole 'nother level.

Kelly looked at Gabby and was greeted by a hard slap. Gabby continued to rain blows on Kelly's head, as she screamed curse words at her with every blow.

"You bitch! You traitor!" Gabby yelled, as Kelly fell backwards from her blows.

Snatching Kelly up, I looked at Gabby and said, "Shut up, bitch! Before you be next". I wasn't sure if I could actually kill her, but I had to say it just to seize the moment, because shit was falling apart.

"Kelly!" I said, yanking her by her shirt. She was an emotional wreck. "Go and grab those pieces of plywood from behind the couch. A hammer should be on my tool rack in the corner over there." I pointed. "Along with a box of nails," I added.

I looked around for something to wrap the officer's body up with. Kelly rushed to grab the items, as I dragged the officer's body by his legs. He was heavy as hell, but my adrenaline was pumping, and with the drugs in my system, I felt like I could drag a horse. I dragged him to the corner and covered him with a blanket. I poured half a bottle of bleach on him to keep the smell down until I could figure out what to do with his body.

Kelly walked over to me with tears streaming down her face. She held a piece of plywood, and the box of nails, along with a hammer. "Kelly, now is not the time to be crying! What's done, is done! What we need to do is, clean this place up, get rid of his car, and pretend he's never been here."

She nodded as she wiped her ongoing tears. I pulled her hand away from her eyes and said, "I'm with you! I'm not going anywhere."

She sniffed, and said, "O—okay." I kissed her hand, and then her lips. "We have to board this window up; that way, she can't alarm anybody else," I said.

Kelly looked over at Gabby, and said, "Why don't we just kill her now? It's all her fault."

"We can't. At least, not right now. She's our leverage, just in case anything happens. She's our hostage!"

## Chapter 20

### Hotboy

"Kuda!" I said, as I stepped in front of Kuda's cell. He was just getting off of work.

"What's up, fam? Everything good?" Kuda asked.

"Naw, but with yo' help, everything will be," I said.

"What you need?" Kuda asked.

"I need you to get me in the back of the infirmary."

"What's in the back of the infirmary?" Kuda asked.

"That's for me to know, and for you to never ask again."

I walked in the infirmary with a mask that covered my nose and mouth. I had on a pair of gloves that made me look like I belonged in the infirmary.

My sharp, freshly made shank was tucked in my waistband; I was on a mission, and nothing could stop me. Kuda led the way, but as soon as we passed the officer's desk, I was on my own. I told Kuda to make sure he stayed close by the C.O., so that he would have an alibi.

"Hey, porter!" a nurse called after me as I walked in the hospice area. I stopped to see what she wanted. "Can I borrow you for a minute? I really need some help."

I followed behind her into the patients' room. There were two patients, one on each side of the room. The nurse walked over to one of the patients as he laid flat on his back. "Can you help me clean him up?"

I looked at the inmate; he had pee running down his leg. He couldn't walk. He had a breathing tube that went through his nose, all the way down his throat. His eyes were open. His right hand—and right leg—was cuffed to the bed rail. Once the inmate saw me, his heart monitor started beeping out of control. He tried to talk, but the tubes prevented every single word.

"Brandon! Calm down, before you give yourself a heart

attack—Acting like you seen a ghost," the nurse said, as she lifted his hospital gown. Brandon looked at me in shock. I looked deeper into his eyes, as I pulled my mask under my lips so that he could see my face. Brandon moved with the little strength he had.

"Brandon, don't make me call for assistance!" the nurse threatened. Brandon's eyes shot open, and he went into a frenzy.

"Give me a second, I'll have to go and get some more help, he don't want to behave today," the nurse said, as she walked out the room.

I peeped out the door to make sure the coast was clear. I pulled out my shank and walked over to Brandon's bed. His eyes widened, and he started pulling at his tubes. "Chill, homie! —Trust me, you better off with me killing you, you don't want to live the rest of yo' life like this," I said. Images of Brandon and Dame jumping Eastwood flashed in my mind. Brandon was the only piece of evidence that could tie us to the murders.

I looked over my shoulder before I raised my shank above my head. His heart monitor went off. The idea came to me. I stashed my shank back in my waistband and walked over to his heart monitor. I unplugged the machine and unplugged his oxygen machine. He gasped, and tried to hold the last bit of oxygen in. I punched him in the stomach, forcing the last bit of air out. I leaned in and whispered, "Tell Dame, I said if I see him in hell, I'ma smash him on sight!"

I snatched Brandon's pillow from under his head and covered his face with it. His legs kicked as he tried to fight for his life. His legs stopped kicking, but I held the pillow over his face just in case he was faking. I lifted the pillow and turned the heart monitor and oxygen machine back on. His heart rate was at zero beats, and he flatlined. I placed his pillow back under his head and walked out unseen.

McFee tried to hold something over my head. He

wasn't shit without his witness. Now that I had him out the way, I could turn up at his expense.

\*\*\*

### Eastwood

I replayed the whole night over in my head a hundred times. Hotboy has been my guy since day one. He was a real nigga. But when you say *was*, does that mean that he ain't no more? My mind was playing tricks on me. I had to blame it on the walls that had me closed in. Being in a cell was already bad as it was. But being in a cell alone—that was devastating! I didn't have any food, or my radio. Bitches wouldn't even give me anything to read. My neighbor snuck me a *Time* magazine. I read the bitch from cover to cover, twice.

"Eastwood!" a porter shouted my name two cells down from me. He pushed the broom in front of my cell and looked in my cell. "Eastwood!" he said.

I nodded. "Yea', what's up?" I asked.

He used the broom to sweep a kite under my cell door. "Hotboy," he said as he walked off, pushing the broom. I snatched the kite up and unfolded the paper.

*"What's good, homie? I hope you back there staying sane. I want you to know I took care of that leftover piece of business. No witnesses! I know the way shit looking, but I want you to know, everything ain't always as they appear. I'm doing everything I can to get you from back there. So bear with me, one love. HB"*

I ripped the kite into pieces and flushed it down the toilet. I had heard the alarm blaring last night. Crazy that the alarm came from Hotboy. I knew the lil' homie was solid. McFee liked to play dangerous games. If dangerous games was what he wanted, then let's play!

# Kingpen

***

## Lt. McFee

"Lieu' are you busy?" Thompson asked me. I excused myself away from the group of nurses.

"Yes, sir," I said, once we were out of earshot. "Do you think this is—him?" Thompson asked.

I nodded and said, "Yes, and I think he's just getting started. You told me to give him free reign to do whatever he wanted, that's exactly what he's going to do."

## Chapter 21

### Newton

*God, why? I know I deserved this, but why did another innocent officer have to die, when he came to save me? God, I just don't understand!* I questioned God for two whole days. The basement had started to smell. I even saw a rat crawl through last night.

Neither Seth nor Kelly had come down here in two days. I heard them pull out the driveway in two different cars, and only one car came back. I'm guessing they actually got rid of the police car. God, I wished they'd got caught. I was hungry as hell. My stomach felt like it was touching my back. I couldn't feel my legs at all anymore. I thought they were just asleep, for me sitting down for so long, but as I tried to move my legs nothing happened.

"Mommy!" Jacob's voice came as a whisper. I thought that I was hearing things, until Jacob crept down the stairs. "Mommy? Are you there?" he asked, as he stood on tiptoe to pull the light string.

"Jacob, baby!" I smiled, as he walked down the steps. As soon as he reached the bottom stairs, he ran over, and hugged me. His arms locked around my neck. "Jacob, I missed you," I said, as I looked him over. "Are you okay? He didn't hurt you, did he? Where is he?" I asked.

"I'm okay, mommy. He's asleep, him and that—mean lady."

"Baby, listen to me, I need you to go! Run next door, and tell them I've been kidnapped, tell them to call the police." I started drifting in an out of consciousness.

"Mommy, are you okay?" Jacob shook me awake. My mouth was dry, my lips were chapped. My words came out as a slur. Jacob had to keep shaking me to keep me awake. "Mommy! Wake up!" he cried.

"Jacob—go—and—get—help!" I said, as my vision

went black.

***

**Seth**

I rolled over and pushed Kelly's arm off of me. Last night, we had some unbelievable sex. We got high and had sex until the sun came up. Kelly showed me some tricks that she could have only learned while turning tricks.

I looked her over as I pulled the covers back, exposing her bare ass. She had a nice shape. I eased out of bed and grabbed my boxers off the floor.

I raised my hands over my head and yawned deep. I was tired as hell. Last night, thanks to the way Kelly put it on me, I finally got some sleep. I had been up for two days straight, stalking the windows. Every time I ducked my head to sniff a line of ice, I thought I heard police sirens outside.

"Jacob!" I shouted, as I walked to his room. He was lying under the blanket. Well, at least I thought he was, until I pulled the cover back. There was two *Iron Man* pillows lined up like a body. "Jacob!" I shouted, as I ran out of his room. I ran straight for the kitchen. The basement door was wide open. The first thing that came to my mind was, Jacob helped Gabby escape. I ran down the stairs at full speed. "Jacob!" I yelled, as Gabby looked at me weakly. "Jacob!" I shouted, as I looked behind the couch for him.

Gabby laughed and said, "I hope he's gone! You didn't deserve to be his father!"

I wanted to slap her because I know she put him up to this. Instead, I ran back up the stairs.

"Jacob! Where are you? You better come out, right now!" I said. I walked in the living room. The front door was wide open, and Jacob stood on the other side with our neighbor.

\*\*\*

### Hotboy

"L.O.P., try this out for me," I said, as I handed L.O.P. a strip of paper rolled up in a piece of Bible paper. I stayed up all night, trying to find something that could hold the K2 spray. I tried using parsley. It held the spray, but it took up too much spray just to make it strong enough to sell. As I was putting the top back on the bottle, I accidently knocked the bottle over, spilling some on a piece of paper. I started to throw it away, but then a thought came to me. If the paper could hold the spray, I could change the dope game.

L.O.P. lit a wick and lit the tip of the Bible paper. "Take it easy! I don't know how strong that shit is!" I warned him as he inhaled the strip.

L.O.P. held his hand up and said, "Youngsta, I've been smoking since you were in diapers." He took a long drag. The Bible paper turned into ashes as his eyes lit up. "Damn!" was all he could say. L.O.P. held on to the door handle as his legs started giving out. He mumbled something as spit spilled out the corner of his mouth.

L.O.P. was the unit dope fiend. Like he said, he had been smoking since I was in diapers. So whenever I had some new shit that I wanted to test, I always brought it to L.O.P., because if he got high, then it had to be some gas, because he didn't just get high off of just anything. The way he was drooling at the mouth, I knew I had my hands on some grade A shit. Now, all I had to do was, get off of it.

"You sho'?" Los asked as I placed another sheet of paper under the nightlight to dry. I had sprayed over twenty sheets, front and back, and I still had a little under a half a bottle left. I was explaining to Los, that this was about to change the whole unit.

"Hell yea'! Look, ain't no dope on the whole unit.

Niggas don't care what they smoke, they just want to get high."

Los brought a piece of paper to his nose and smelled it. "So how you gon' sell it?"

I smiled. "You like that, huh? Can't smell shit, can you?" He shook his head. I sprayed another sheet of paper and answered his question. "I'm gon' charge seven hundred for a whole sheet." I held up my ID and said, "I'm gon' charge a hundred for an ID size."

Los laughed. "My nigga, ain't nobody gon' pay for no fucking paper."

"Watch!" I said.

By the end of the night, I had sold fifteen sheets, and twenty ID's. Niggas was tryna pay me to give them the game on what I had sprayed it with. One nigga even offered me two racks. I turned him down, and went and sold four sheets, and made over four racks. I kept it playa and gave all my day one niggas a playa deal. Instead of charging them seven hundred like I charged everybody else, I charged them five hundred. In twenty-four hours, I had made over fifteen thousand, and the smokers were loving it. They wasn't feeling it at first because it was actually paper that they were smoking. But, once they felt the high, they had no more complaints.

The hustlers was loving it, too. Paying seven hundred for a piece of paper seemed extreme. Once they calculated how many ID's they were able to cut out, they ended up with a five-hundred-dollar profit; six hundred, if you knew how to cut it right.

I looked at Los and laughed. "What you got to say now?" I asked him as he made another sell.

"You the man!" He laughed. "So what's next?" he asked.

"The final stage. Go home, one way, or another."

## Chapter 22

### Lt. McFee

"Lieu', we have another man down," Sergeant Childs said, as I watched two nurses wheel an inmate down the hall on a gurney to medical. That was the third inmate in the last twenty minutes. Just earlier, we had to carry one to medical in a restraint bag. The inmate was kicking and screaming, like he was seeing ghosts.

"Where at?" I asked

"H—Henry," Sergeant Childs said.

Kingsley's wing. It had been two days since I gave Kingsley the bottle of K2 spray. He didn't waste any time putting it to use. O.I.G Thompson was actually impressed with the constant K2 attacks that the inmates were having. Me, on the other hand, I wasn't impressed. K2 attacks didn't arouse me. Especially when I knew I was the cause of the attacks. What aroused me was, when I ran down on a dirty inmate. The looks on their faces when they were caught red-handed, that's what aroused me. Every inmate felt like they had the game figured out. They felt like they were smarter than us, by a mile. Especially with most of us officers being from a small town. So when a country bumpkin like myself ran down on them, it was like sex on the beach. Except now, I couldn't run down on the inmate that was causing all the ruckus, because I had already gave him free will. I felt like how God felt when he gave Adam and Eve freewill in the Garden of Eden. As soon as I gave Kingsley free will to do whatever he wanted, I wanted to take it back.

"Lieutenant on the wing!" an inmate shouted from the dayroom, as I walked on H-wing with Sergeant Childs, and two female nurses. The run was deserted, except for the inmate that had the K2 attack. The inmate that had the K2 attack was lying on the floor, in a pool of his own vomit.

He wasn't screaming, like the other inmates that we previously took to medical, but he had the same habit of kicking his feet.

"I was finishing up my house call—I came down the front half of the stairs and saw two inmates carrying him to his cell," the C.O. working the wing explained. "I asked them what was wrong with him, they didn't answer. The inmate started laughing, next thing you know, he's throwing up."

"Take him to the infirmary, while I take a look around," I said to Sergeant Childs. I headed down one row as another inmate yelled that I was coming. As I walked down the run, I looked in every cell. I got halfway down the run and saw an inmate in his cell sitting on his toilet, slumped. He had his head down as his chin rested on his chest. I hit the cell bars with my flashlight. The inmate wiped the spit from his mouth and looked up. As soon as he saw who I was, he got his shit together quick.

Walking up the back half of the stairs, an inmate alarmed the rest of the inmates that I was on two row. I was used to them "holding security" for each other. What boggled me was, when someone held security, and I still walk up and catch somebody doing something that they know they ain't got no business doing.

Everything on two row looked in order. But I didn't care; nonetheless, I was determined to get to three row. I took the front half of three row steps two at a time. The same inmate yelled that I was on three row. Where I was headed, I knew he couldn't hear the warning from where his cell was. A few small "spy" mirrors crept out the bars. They yanked them back in their cells as they saw me getting closer to their cells. As I walked by their cells, they all of a sudden seemed to be asleep. And they wondered why they were in prison. There was no such thing as a smart criminal.

"Um, huhh!" I cleared my throat as I walked in front of Kingsley's cell. I got lucky that his celly wasn't in the cell with him. Kingsley placed his finger to his lips as he tucked some papers under his mattress.

"I see you doing exactly what I asked you to do," I said, as I looked to see if anyone was in the cell next door.

"What the fuck you doing? —You can't just be popping up here like this!—Niggas already thinking I'ma snitch, you adding fuel to the fire," he said as he flushed the toilet to drown our conversation out from anyone that could be listening.

"I just wanted to make sure we're on the same page. I give you what you want, and you give me what I want."

"You can't see what's going on? Niggas is around this bitch flopping like fish. My end of the deal is good, you just make sure my homie don't go down for that dope, or that false ass murder you tryna pin on us."

I laughed as he still pretended he had nothing to do with the murders. The only witness we had died in the infirmary all of a sudden. I guarantee he had something to do with that, too.

"I'm a man of my word," I said, as I pulled another bottle of K2 spray from my pocket. O.I.G Thompson said that this kind was actually stronger then the last kind.

I tossed the bottle to him and said, "Have fun! But not too much fun."

I started to walk away, until I saw a few mirrors looking at me. "Let me have your speaker—We have company," I said, as I put my hand through the bars.

He unplugged the cord from the back of the radio. "How did you know I had one?" he asked, as he handed me the cardboard speaker.

"I heard the static in your radio when I walked up. I ain't green as y'all think I am!"

# Kingpen

## Chapter 23

### Seth

I sighed as I tossed another cigarette out the window. Instead of working in the building, they had me working the perimeter. Meaning I had to drive around the unit in circles, lucky me! Lately, I've been beyond stressed. My life has been nothing but negative energy to get my revenge on Gabby and Kingsley. It's been a revenge that I regret. It's taking a toll on me for the worse. I killed a man, for a woman that only wants to sniff all of my dope. My son, he's afraid of me. Just the other day, he snuck out the house and went over to the neighbor's house, telling them that I hurt his mom. When my neighbor told me that, I sent Jacob to his room. I showed my neighbor Kelly, who she thought was Gabby asleep in the bed. I apologized for the misunderstanding and sent her on her merry.

"Major Burts, to Officer Kiles!" my radio sounded off. I picked the walkie-talkie up and said, "This is officer Kiles."

The radio stayed silent for a second. "Just making sure you're awake," the Major said.

Hell yea', I was awake. I was wide awake. I was already on my third line of ice, and my shift had just really started. "Yes, sir! I'm about to pull around to the front right now," I said, as I made a right turn.

"I need you to do an escort—We have another inmate that needs a transport to the hospital," the Major said.

"On my way," I said. I pulled around to the parking lot and parked. I doubled checked my nose to make sure I didn't leave any residue. The Major met me at the front gate to retrieve the TDCJ-issued pistol.

"Where is your mask?" he asked, like he was my father. I pulled it out my back pocket and showed it to him. "Put it on! —And keep it on!—This corona shit is not a game," he said.

"Am I going alone?" I asked.

"Yes, but once you get there, you'll be bringing another officer back," he said.

"Yes, sir," I said, as I walked away like I was in a hurry to get the job done. I was really just tryna get away from him. If I could smell the dope coming through my pores, then I know he could too. Good thing he had a mask on.

I was going to stop at the corner store on my way back and get another pack of cigarettes. I needed to stop. If the stress didn't give me heart attack first, the cigarettes would definitely take me out.

"Kiles, are you okay?" the Major asked as I stopped, making him walk into the back of me. The perfect plan came to mind. I finally found out how I was going to kill Kingsley!

\*\*\*

**Hotboy**

**Three days later—**

"Kingsley!" a C.O. called my name for mail. I was watching the news as the whole dayroom watched in amazement as the death toll went up by another hundred thousand..

"Kingsley?" the C.O. asked as I went to the bars to grab my mail.

"Yes," I said, as he handed me a piece of mail. I looked at the name on the envelope. It was from the parole board. I went to the other side of the dayroom and put my back against the wall. I opened the envelope and read the letter:

*Pursuant to the Presiding Officer's Temporary Order, all in-person Unit Parole interviews conducted by an*

*Institutional Parole Officer will be temporarily suspended. By this letter you are being notified that your case was assigned to an Institutional Parole Officer, and, after reviewing your file, we will remain you in custody for another five years. After that, you will be brought up again for another parole hearing.*
*Signed,*
*The Texas Board of Pardons and Parole.*

I went to the toilet and flushed the letter. I pretended like I was peeing and let out a few tears. I washed my hands and wiped my face to hide the tears. I couldn't believe them ho's set me off, and for five more years. That's like a whole 'nother sentence. Them bitches didn't even have the decency to tell me in person. Five more years. I wasn't going to do five more years, so that they could set me off again. Or worse, I have to kill another nigga, and never see daylight again. I was going to get the fuck out of here. By any means!

\*\*\*

## Lt. McFee

"Have a seat, Lieu," O.I.G Thompson said, as he walked around his desk.

"You're doing an amazing job. My boss has noticed the drug flow going through the unit. He's been blowing my phone up looking for some answers. I told him that I have everything under control. I made him a promise, that I would deliver him the inmate responsible for the recent murders, as well as the inmate that's responsible for the drug flow. As soon as I hand him Kingsley on a silver platter, this—" he motioned around the office with his hand— "will be yours."

I guess Thompson thought I was green too. His whole

conversation was, 'I—I—I!' He probably never told his boss about me. He was just using me, like he always did. Since day one, I've been his do-boy. Do this, do that! I had something for him though.

"I don't know what to say," I said.

"Say *thank you!*"

"Thank you, sir! For everything! You have no idea how grateful I am. I can't wait to take him down, and everyone that's associated with him!"

\*\*\*

## Hotboy

I walked in the chow hall on another level. Ever since the set-off, I've been going through the motions. My expectations were so high on going home, but they shot me down.

"Kingsley!" I heard my name being called. I kept walking with my head down.

"Kingsley! Are you okay?" I turned around to see who was calling my name.

"Kiles, what the fuck do you want?" I asked. I wasn't in the mood to be fucked with.

"I haven't seen you in a while. You good? You look down." He sounded like he really cared. He probably ran out of dope and needs my help to get some more. I told him he would be back.

"I'm good, homie, ain't nothing I can't handle." I said, as I walked away.

"I can't tell," he said, walking behind me.

I stopped in my tracks. I was looking for a fight and I didn't care who it was with. A C.O. or another inmate. Somebody was gon' feel my pain.

"Mind yo' buisness! This ain't what you want." I faced him.

He took a step back and said, "I'm not the enemy, remember. I'm on yo' side."

He was right. I was tripping. Ever since Eastwood got jammed up, and I got set-off, I've been on the edge, just waiting on someone to push me. I couldn't get my mind off of escaping. I wasn't tryna do another day in here, let alone five more years.

"My bad, homie. Shit's just been fucking with me." I sat on top of the table.

"Shit. Like what?" he asked.

"I got a five-year set-off," I said, as I shook my head. "Bitches gave me a fucking set-off," I said, as reality hit me.

"Damn, that's a whole 'nother sentence!" he said.

"Exactly!"

"So, what you gon' do?" he asked.

"I don't know. But, I ain't finna stay here." I sighed.

"What you gon' do? Go to another unit?" he asked.

"Naw. I'm gon' get the fuck out of prison altogether. I'm gon' escape." My mind was made up. I wasn't staying in here any longer.

"Escaping. Man, stop. The last person that tried to escape, he got shot, and now he's in a wheelchair, permanently. These people are trained to kill people that try to escape."

What he said went in one ear, and out the other. "I'll take my chances," I said, as I stood up.

"Do you even have a plan?" he asked.

"Yea', get out, by any means. I'll go to Mexico if I have to. I ain't staying, I know that. With all the money that I made in here, I can go to Mexico, and live lavish."

"How much?" he asked out the blue.

"How much, what?"

"How much will you pay me, to help you escape?" he

said, catching me by surprise.

"How much you looking for?"

"Let's just say, I got the perfect plan, and the perfect route. But, in order for it to work, I'll need ten grand sent to my cash app, and for you to listen very closely."

I listened to Kiles explain his plan. It was beyond perfect. One that I wouldn't have thought of. I guess he wasn't as green as I thought he was!

\*\*\*

### Lt. McFee

"Mr. Thompson, Can I speak with you for a second?" I asked Thompson, as I caught him walking into his office.

He unlocked the door and escorted me in. "Yes," he said, as he went to his mini fridge. He grabbed two bottles of water and tossed me one.

"Sir, I think this is going too far. Not only are some inmates dying, but we now have some officers experimenting with the drug."

"McFee, I don't care if the warden smokes it. What I need is for this place to look like hell, so that the district would want to shut us down; that way, I can come in and save the day. I'll get a promotion, and everything else wouldn't matter."

A knock came at the door.

"Come in!" he said.

I looked back to see Kingsley walk through the door with both of his hands behind his back. "Who authorized you to come to my office?" Thompson asked.

"No one!" Kingsley said, "I came to make a deal." he said.

"A deal?" Thompson said, taken aback.

"Yea'," Kingsley said.

Thompson stood up and said, "I don't deal with

criminals."

Kingsley pulled out a bottle of K2 spray and tossed it to Thompson. "How about now?" Kingsley said.

"What's that?" Thompson said, like he never saw it before.

"That's yours, isn't it?" Kingsley shot back.

"Lieutenant, what is this inmate speaking of?" Thompson asked me.

"Sir—I—I don't know." I played dumb.

Kingsley got upset. "You know what I'm talking about. You said that the O.I.G sent this to me to sell, in exchange for immunity. What I'm trying to see is, what's taking so long?" Kingsley spat.

Thompson looked at me and said, "You know, good peasant! You weren't supposed to say my name! You can't do shit right! That's why you'll never get my job, you can't follow orders! You don't deserve my job, let alone the bars on your shirt. You should get demoted, and put in the kitchen, with the rest of your kind." He walked around his desk and stood face to face with Kingsley. "Immunity my ass! You're never going to go home if I have anything to do with it. So, what? Yea', you got set up. Yea', I had you sell poison to the whole unit! It was all for a purpose, a greater purpose. See, drugs control the population. Yea', y'all have K2 attacks, but it's less killing going on. Y'all are always too high to do anything but eat and sleep. That's why I'm the best man to run this district, because I'll have this place like a prison is supposed to look!"

"Sir, so you're saying, this whole time, you used me?" I asked.

"How could I use you, when you're not worth a shit! You used yourself! You want my job, but you don't deserve it! You don't have the balls that this job requires! I give you one simple task, give this little shit as much dope as you can to make the unit look like hell, and you can't even do that right! You went and told him, I sent it to him. How dumb can you be!"

Kingsley eyed the bottle of K2 spray.

"Don't worry, Kingsley!" Thompson said, as he watched him look at the spray. "I'm going to make sure you go down for those murders in the shower, as well as the drug flow on the unit. You can tell them whatever you want, they'll never believe you! I'm a man of the law, I have a badge. All you have is a number!"

I stood up and smiled. "Thank you, sir!" I said, as I looked at Thompson. The door opened, and a dozen police officers ran inside.

"Jared Thompson, you have the right to remain silent—" an officer read him his rights, as they placed him in cuffs.

"You bitch! You fucking snitch! I knew I shouldn't have put you under my wing, you weren't nothing like me!" Thompson said, as they escorted him out the office. "You will pay! Both of you!" Thompson kept screaming until his voice disappeared

"Mr. Kingsley, I want to thank you, for doing the right thing," McFee said.

"I don't care about you, or him. All I care about is—"

I cut him off. "I know, I know! Your friend will be out today, and don't worry about any further charges coming your way. I'll take care of it."

Kingsley smiled. Then as soon as his smile came, it faded. He grabbed at his heart as if it was about to come out of his chest. He fell down to one knee and held on to the side of the desk for support.

"Kingsley! Are you okay?" I asked, as he panted for air.

"My—my—" he said, before falling over.

"I need medical assistance; we have an inmate down!" I shouted in my walkie-talkie. "Help is on the way! Just stay with me!"

***

## Hotboy

"Help is on the way! Just stay with me!" McFee's voice echoed in my head as I lay on the floor. Two male nurses picked me up and laid me on a gurney.

"We can't take him to the infirmary; we have too many positive corona cases—We have to transport him to the hospital," one of the nurses said to McFee.

"Lieutenent McFee, to transport!" he spoke in his walkie-talkie.

"Transport, this is Kiles."

"Meet us at the back dock in a medical van," McFee said.

"Copy!"

The double doors slammed, and McFee slapped the van with his hand for the driver to pull off. The van drove to the main gate, as another officer checked the van for anything out of the usual. "ID's please?" the officer asked the driver, and the passenger seat rider. "Kiles, Grain," the officer read the names from their ID's and handed them back to them. The van pulled off again past the gate.

"Almost," Kiles said.

We rode for another five minutes before anyone spoke again. "We're good—For now," Kiles said.

I sat up and removed the IV from my arm. Grain rushed to the back seat and kissed me like she missed me. "See, I told you I'll break you out!" she said, as she kissed me again.

Kiles stayed quiet, as he looked through the rearview mirror at us. He drove at a steady speed as he kept looking to see if anyone was following us. "They won't report the van missing until another thirty minutes," Kiles said. "By that time, you'll be long gone—You and Gabriela!" he added.

"Who's Gabriela?" Grain asked.

I jumped up and tried to move. The medicine that the nurses injected in me had me drowsy as hell, so I thought I was moving fast, but I was really moving slow.

Kiles jerked the steering wheel, causing me and Grain to fall.

"Kiles, what the fuck!" Grain yelled, as she helped me up. "Shut up, bitch! I'm saving you from him! Ask him, who is Gabriela!" Kiles spat, as he drove recklessly.

"Don't listen to him," I slurred.

Kiles slowed down and pulled a revolver from out the glove department. Pointing the gun at me, he said, "Tell her!"

Grain screamed as she saw the gun. "Kiles, wait! Put the gun down, before somebody get hurt!" she said.

"Too late! He hurt me a long time ago, when he slept with my fiancée, and ruined my life."

I knew it all along. My conscious had warned me, but I didn't listen. I knew they were connected in some way, but I didn't expect it to be his fiancée.

"Gianni, tell me he's lying!" Grain said.

I couldn't lie to her. She had went out her way to help me escape. I owed her the truth. "I'm sorry!" I managed to say. "It was way before me and you. I didn't know either of you at that time."

Kiles made a sharp right, tossing Grain in my lap.

"Babe, I'm sorry," I said, as I tried to hold her. She moved my arms from around her and held on the gurney for support.

"Kiles, where are you taking us?" she asked.

"I'm taking him to his babymama, so they can die together," he said, as he sped up. We drove for another ten minutes before the van finally stopped.

"Get out!" Kiles spat, as he pointed his pistol at us. I was still a little drowsy, but I could walk now.

"Kiles, bruh, this is between me and you—Just let her go, she's innocent in all of this," I said.

"Nobody is going anywhere! —We're just about to surprise Gabby, that's all!" he said, as he killed the engine. He stepped out the van, and opened the double doors. "Get out!" he shouted.

Grain stepped out first, and she helped me step down. As soon as my foot touched the ground, Kiles snatched me up by my shirt. "One false move, and I will kill you! You better ask your homeboy, Dub. Oh wait, you can't." He laughed.

I wanted to spit on him. He was a gangsta with that gun, but a bitch without it. He killed Dub, so I knew he wouldn't hesitate to kill me to.

The front door opened to a house, and a woman stepped out in some jean shorts and a tank top. "Seth, what the fuck! Who are they?" the woman asked.

Kiles shoved us towards the front door. "Get the hell in the damn house! Don't ask me shit!" Kiles spat, as he held the gun at my back.

Once we were inside, Kiles slammed the door behind us. Kiles spoke to the woman. "Go pack some things we can use. As soon as I'm finished, we're leaving."

The woman rushed off to the back room.

"Let's go!" Kiles said, shoving me to the kitchen. "Downstairs, now!" he shouted. I hesitated. I knew this was my last chance. Going down those stairs, would only seal my fate. Damn, I should've stayed in prison.

"Kiles, man, let her go, please. She ain't got nothing to do with nothing. She ain't gon' say anything. She can't, 'cause she helped you help me escape."

"Either you get down those stairs, or I kill her right now. Your choice."

I walked down the steps, fearing what would happen when I made it to the bottom. A bright light shone above my head, as Kiles pulled a string. The sight in front of me was devastating.

"Gabby!" I said.

# Kingpen

# Chapter 24

### Newton

The basement door opened, and the light from the kitchen looked like the glowing light from heaven. A male figure walked down the steps, with a woman behind him. For a moment, I thought it was Seth and Kelly. When the light turned on, I thought I was dreaming. It was Gianni, another woman, and Seth. Gianni still looked good. He looked a little sluggish, but he looked good.

"Gabby!" Gianni said, once he saw me. Tears formed in the corner of his eyes. It was the first time he's seen me since the night I was shoved over three row, and I looked like shit. "What did you do to her?" he asked Seth.

"The same thing I'm going to do to you," Seth said, as he fired off a shot, hitting Gianni in his right shoulder. The woman that they came with them screamed, and she covered her mouth with her hand.

"You piece of shit!" Gianni said, as he held his shoulder in pain.

"Tell me something I don't know!" Seth said, as he squatted down in front of Gianni. "Tell me why you picked my fiancée, of all the women on the unit? You could've had any woman you wanted, but you picked mine!" Seth screamed, as Kelly walked down the basement stairs. Seth squeezed the trigger again, shooting Gianni in his chest. The gun echoed throughout the basement.

Gianni's blood dripped from the corner of his mouth as he tried to speak. "Bruh—I didn't mean to—" Gianni said, as he wiped the blood from his mouth. "I didn't mean to come between y'all," he managed to say.

Tears fell from my eyes, as I watched Gianni's life slip away from him. He was barely able to move, as he tried to stand up.

Seth looked at him in amazement. Gianni wasn't going

to die on his knees.

"Kiles, please! Don't kill him, please!" the woman that came with them begged.

Kelly walked behind Seth and whispered something in his ear. "Okay," Seth said to Kelly. "Take everything to the car," he added.

"Jacob!" Kelly said, as she turned to see Jacob holding a gun in his tiny hands. "Baby, what are you doing with that?" Kelly asked.

"Mommy!" Jacob said, as the gun shook in his hands.

"Yes!" Kelly smiled, as she walked up to Jacob. "I'm your mother." she said.

Jacob's innocent face changed as Kelly walked up to him. She touched his face gently with the palm of her hand and said, "Jacob, I'm your mother."

The gun went off, startling us all. "No, you're not!" Jacob said as the gun fell from his hand.

As soon as Kelly's body dropped, Gianni was all over Seth. Seth had the upper hand, because Gianni was injured, but Gianni wasn't going down without a fight. Seth was getting the best of him, until the other woman jumped on Seth's back. "Ahhh, bitch!" Seth yelled as the woman bit his cheek.

Seth slung her over his head, as blood covered his cheek. Jacob looked on in shock, seeing his father bleeding from his cheek. Seth pointed the gun at Gianni and let off another shot; this time he missed. He let off another shot, catching him in his leg, forcing Gianni to fall to the ground. Gianni raised one hand as if he could block the next bullet.

"Seth—please!" I begged, as Seth aimed the gun at Gianni's head. Seth looked at me and spat. "Fuck you, and him!" Seth said, as his finger went to the trigger.

The gun sounded, but Gianni didn't get hit. Seth looked at his chest as blood changed the color of his shirt. Seth fell down to one knee as he looked at me. A tear fell down his cheek. He looked beyond tired. He gasped one last time as his body fell over.

"Gianni!" the woman said, as she ran over to Gianni with the gun still in her hand.

Gianni was laid out on his back. His breathing had slowed down, but he was alive. "Grain—tha—thank, you!" he said.

She cried and said, "I tol' you, stop calling me that— You know my name," she said.

Gianni managed to smile. "You kept your word—You got me out," he said.

I watched them interact like I wasn't there. They looked like they were in a movie, doing a romantic love scene. Their love for each other was visible and genuine. I felt a pang of jealousy, seeing the way she held Gianni's head on her lap. "You hear that, babe?" Grain said, as the sound of police sirens could be heard.

"I'm not going back to prison," Gianni said. "I'd rather die!" he spat.

"You can't babe, you can't leave me. I'm pregnant!" Grain surprised him.

Gianni looked up with tears of joy in his eyes. "You serious?" he asked.

She nodded and said, "It's a boy!"

Gianni looked at me, and said to Grain, "We're naming him Gianni Kingsley, the third."

Grain looked at him, confused. "The third? I didn't know you're a junior."

"I'm not—But I had a son, and his name was Gianni junior," he said.

The basement door swung open, and a gang of police officers ran down the steps with their guns drawn. One of them swept Jacob up in his arms and carried him up the stairs.

"Gianni Kingsley!" one of the officers said to Gianni.

Gianni smiled and said, "McFee, how did you find me?"

"The van has a tracking device—We knew where you were all along," McFee said.

"Did you let my homie out of lock up?" Gianni asked. McFee nodded and said, "Yes, he's waiting on you to come back. He's on the wing, same cell as before."

"I'm not going back—I'm tired—I haven't rested in a long time—I think I deserve some rest," Gianni said, as he gasped. His head laid still on Grain's leg, as she burst in tears.

"Gianni! Wake up! You can't leave me!" she cried.

Gianni took his last breath as a man in chains. He was now a free man. By any means necessary!

**The End**

## Submission Guideline

Submit the first three chapters of your completed manuscript to ldpsubmissions@gmail.com, subject line: Your book's title. The manuscript must be in a .doc file and sent as an attachment. Document should be in Times New Roman, double spaced and in size 12 font. Also, provide your synopsis and full contact information. If sending multiple submissions, they must each be in a separate email.

Have a story but no way to send it electronically? You can still submit to LDP/Ca$h Presents. Send in the first three chapters, written or typed, of your completed manuscript to:

**LDP: Submissions Dept**
**Po Box 944**
**Stockbridge, Ga 30281**

*DO NOT send original manuscript. Must be a duplicate.*

Provide your synopsis and a cover letter containing your full contact information.

Thanks for considering LDP and Ca$h Presents.

# Kingpen

**Coming Soon from Lock Down Publications/Ca$h Presents**

BOW DOWN TO MY GANGSTA

By **Ca$h**

TORN BETWEEN TWO

By **Coffee**

THE STREETS STAINED MY SOUL **II**

By **Marcellus Allen**

BLOOD OF A BOSS **VI**

SHADOWS OF THE GAME II

TRAP BASTARD II

By **Askari**

LOYAL TO THE GAME **IV**

By **T.J. & Jelissa**

IF LOVING YOU IS WRONG… **III**

By **Jelissa**

TRUE SAVAGE **VIII**

MIDNIGHT CARTEL IV

DOPE BOY MAGIC IV

CITY OF KINGZ III

By **Chris Green**

BLAST FOR ME **III**

A SAVAGE DOPEBOY III

CUTTHROAT MAFIA III

DUFFLE BAG CARTEL VI

HEARTLESS GOON VI

By **Ghost**

A HUSTLER'S DECEIT III

KILL ZONE **II**

BAE BELONGS TO ME III

# Concrete Killa 2

A DOPE BOY'S QUEEN III

By **Aryanna**

COKE KINGS V

KING OF THE TRAP III

By **T.J. Edwards**

GORILLAZ IN THE BAY V

3X KRAZY III

**De'Kari**

THE STREETS ARE CALLING II

**Duquie Wilson**

KINGPIN KILLAZ IV

STREET KINGS III

PAID IN BLOOD III

CARTEL KILLAZ IV

DOPE GODS III

**Hood Rich**

SINS OF A HUSTLA II

**ASAD**

KINGZ OF THE GAME VI

**Playa Ray**

SLAUGHTER GANG IV

RUTHLESS HEART IV

**By Willie Slaughter**

FUK SHYT II

**By Blakk Diamond**

TRAP QUEEN

RICH $AVAGE II

**By Troublesome**

YAYO V

GHOST MOB II

# Kingpen

# Concrete Killa 2

THE STREETS MADE ME III

By **Larry D. Wright**

IF YOU CROSS ME ONCE II

ANGEL III

By **Anthony Fields**

FRIEND OR FOE III

By **Mimi**

SAVAGE STORMS III

By **Meesha**

BLOOD ON THE MONEY III

**By J-Blunt**

THE STREETS WILL NEVER CLOSE II

**By K'ajji**

NIGHTMARES OF A HUSTLA III

**By King Dream**

IN THE ARM OF HIS BOSS

**By Jamila**

HARD AND RUTHLESS II

**By Von Wiley Hall**

LEVELS TO THIS SHYT II

**By Ah'Million**

MOB TIES III

**By SayNoMore**

BODYMORE MURDERLAND II

**By Delmont Player**

THE LAST OF THE OGS III

**Tranay Adams**

FOR THE LOVE OF A BOSS II

**By C. D. Blue**

# Kingpen

## Available Now

RESTRAINING ORDER **I & II**
By **CA$H & Coffee**
LOVE KNOWS NO BOUNDARIES **I II & III**
By **Coffee**
RAISED AS A GOON I, II, III & IV
BRED BY THE SLUMS I, II, III
BLAST FOR ME I & II
ROTTEN TO THE CORE I II III
A BRONX TALE I, II, III
DUFFLE BAG CARTEL I II III IV V
HEARTLESS GOON I II III IV V
A SAVAGE DOPEBOY I II
DRUG LORDS I II III
CUTTHROAT MAFIA I II
By **Ghost**
LAY IT DOWN **I & II**
LAST OF A DYING BREED I II
BLOOD STAINS OF A SHOTTA I & II III
By **Jamaica**
LOYAL TO THE GAME I II III
LIFE OF SIN I, II III
By **TJ & Jelissa**
BLOODY COMMAS I & II
SKI MASK CARTEL I II & III
KING OF NEW YORK I II,III IV V
RISE TO POWER I II III

# Concrete Killa 2

COKE KINGS I II III IV
BORN HEARTLESS I II III IV
KING OF THE TRAP I II
By **T.J. Edwards**
IF LOVING HIM IS WRONG…I & II
LOVE ME EVEN WHEN IT HURTS I II III
By **Jelissa**
WHEN THE STREETS CLAP BACK I & II III
THE HEART OF A SAVAGE I II III
By **Jibril Williams**
A DISTINGUISHED THUG STOLE MY HEART I II & III
LOVE SHOULDN'T HURT I II III IV
RENEGADE BOYS I II III IV
PAID IN KARMA I II III
SAVAGE STORMS I II
By **Meesha**
A GANGSTER'S CODE I &, II III
A GANGSTER'S SYN I II III
THE SAVAGE LIFE I II III
CHAINED TO THE STREETS I II III
BLOOD ON THE MONEY I II
**By J-Blunt**
PUSH IT TO THE LIMIT
By **Bre' Hayes**
BLOOD OF A BOSS **I, II, III, IV, V**
SHADOWS OF THE GAME
TRAP BASTARD
By **Askari**
THE STREETS BLEED MURDER **I, II & III**
THE HEART OF A GANGSTA I II& III

# Kingpen

By **Jerry Jackson**

CUM FOR ME I II III IV V VI VII

An **LDP Erotica Collaboration**

BRIDE OF A HUSTLA **I  II & II**

THE FETTI GIRLS **I, II& III**

CORRUPTED BY A GANGSTA I, II III, IV

BLINDED BY HIS LOVE

THE PRICE YOU PAY FOR LOVE I II

DOPE GIRL MAGIC I II III

By **Destiny Skai**

WHEN A GOOD GIRL GOES BAD

By **Adrienne**

THE COST OF LOYALTY I II III

**By Kweli**

A GANGSTER'S REVENGE **I II III & IV**

THE BOSS MAN'S DAUGHTERS I II III IV V

A SAVAGE LOVE **I & II**

BAE BELONGS TO ME I II

A HUSTLER'S DECEIT I, II, III

WHAT BAD BITCHES DO I, II, III

SOUL OF A MONSTER I II III

KILL ZONE

A DOPE BOY'S QUEEN I II

By **Aryanna**

A KINGPIN'S AMBITON

A KINGPIN'S AMBITION **II**

I MURDER FOR THE DOUGH

By **Ambitious**

TRUE SAVAGE I II III IV V VI VII

DOPE BOY MAGIC I, II, III

# Concrete Killa 2

MIDNIGHT CARTEL I II III

CITY OF KINGZ I II

By **Chris Green**

A DOPEBOY'S PRAYER

By **Eddie "Wolf" Lee**

THE KING CARTEL **I, II & III**

By **Frank Gresham**

THESE NIGGAS AIN'T LOYAL **I, II & III**

By **Nikki Tee**

GANGSTA SHYT **I II &III**

By **CATO**

THE ULTIMATE BETRAYAL

By **Phoenix**

BOSS'N UP **I , II & III**

By **Royal Nicole**

I LOVE YOU TO DEATH

**By Destiny J**

I RIDE FOR MY HITTA

I STILL RIDE FOR MY HITTA

By **Misty Holt**

LOVE & CHASIN' PAPER

By **Qay Crockett**

TO DIE IN VAIN

SINS OF A HUSTLA

By **ASAD**

BROOKLYN HUSTLAZ

By **Boogsy Morina**

BROOKLYN ON LOCK I & II

By **Sonovia**

GANGSTA CITY

# Kingpen

By **Teddy Duke**

A DRUG KING AND HIS DIAMOND I & II III

A DOPEMAN'S RICHES

HER MAN, MINE'S TOO I, II

CASH MONEY HO'S

THE WIFEY I USED TO BE I II

By **Nicole Goosby**

TRAPHOUSE KING **I II & III**

KINGPIN KILLAZ I II III

STREET KINGS I II

PAID IN BLOOD **I II**

CARTEL KILLAZ I II III

DOPE GODS I II

By **Hood Rich**

LIPSTICK KILLAH **I, II, III**

CRIME OF PASSION I II & III

FRIEND OR FOE I II

By **Mimi**

STEADY MOBBN' **I, II, III**

THE STREETS STAINED MY SOUL

By **Marcellus Allen**

WHO SHOT YA **I, II, III**

SON OF A DOPE FIEND I II

HEAVEN GOT A GHETTO

**Renta**

GORILLAZ IN THE BAY **I II III IV**

TEARS OF A GANGSTA I II

3X KRAZY I II

**DE'KARI**

TRIGGADALE I II III

# Concrete Killa 2

**Elijah R. Freeman**

GOD BLESS THE TRAPPERS I, II, III

THESE SCANDALOUS STREETS I, II, III

FEAR MY GANGSTA I, II, III IV, V

THESE STREETS DON'T LOVE NOBODY I, II

BURY ME A G I, II, III, IV, V

A GANGSTA'S EMPIRE I, II, III, IV

THE DOPEMAN'S BODYGAURD I II

THE REALEST KILLAZ I II III

THE LAST OF THE OGS I II

**Tranay Adams**

THE STREETS ARE CALLING

**Duquie Wilson**

MARRIED TO A BOSS... I II III

**By Destiny Skai & Chris Green**

KINGZ OF THE GAME I II III IV V

**Playa Ray**

SLAUGHTER GANG I II III

RUTHLESS HEART I II III

**By Willie Slaughter**

FUK SHYT

**By Blakk Diamond**

DON'T F#CK WITH MY HEART I II

**By Linnea**

ADDICTED TO THE DRAMA I II III

IN THE ARM OF HIS BOSS II

**By Jamila**

YAYO I II III IV

A SHOOTER'S AMBITION I II

**By S. Allen**

# Kingpen

TRAP GOD I II III

RICH $AVAGE

**By Troublesome**

FOREVER GANGSTA

GLOCKS ON SATIN SHEETS I II

**By Adrian Dulan**

TOE TAGZ I II III

LEVELS TO THIS SHYT

**By Ah'Million**

KINGPIN DREAMS I II III

**By Paper Boi Rari**

CONFESSIONS OF A GANGSTA I II III

**By Nicholas Lock**

I'M NOTHING WITHOUT HIS LOVE

SINS OF A THUG

TO THE THUG I LOVED BEFORE

**By Monet Dragun**

CAUGHT UP IN THE LIFE I II III

**By Robert Baptiste**

NEW TO THE GAME I II III

MONEY, MURDER & MEMORIES I II III

By **Malik D. Rice**

LIFE OF A SAVAGE I II III

A GANGSTA'S QUR'AN I II III

MURDA SEASON I II III

GANGLAND CARTEL I II III

CHI'RAQ GANGSTAS I II III

KILLERS ON ELM STREET I II

JACK BOYZ N DA BRONX

A DOPEBOY'S DREAM

By **Romell Tukes**

LOYALTY AIN'T PROMISED I II

**By Keith Williams**

QUIET MONEY I II III

THUG LIFE I II III

EXTENDED CLIP I II

By **Trai'Quan**

THE STREETS MADE ME I II

By **Larry D. Wright**

THE ULTIMATE SACRIFICE I, II, III, IV, V, VI

KHADIFI

IF YOU CROSS ME ONCE

ANGEL I II

By **Anthony Fields**

THE LIFE OF A HOOD STAR

**By Ca$h & Rashia Wilson**

THE STREETS WILL NEVER CLOSE

**By K'ajji**

CREAM I II

**By Yolanda Moore**

NIGHTMARES OF A HUSTLA I II

**By King Dream**

CONCRETE KILLA I II

**By Kingpen**

HARD AND RUTHLESS

**By Von Wiley Hall**

GHOST MOB II

**Stilloan Robinson**

MOB TIES I II

# Kingpen

**By SayNoMore**
BODYMORE MURDERLAND
**By Delmont Player**
FOR THE LOVE OF A BOSS
**By C. D. Blue**

**BOOKS BY LDP'S CEO, CA$H**

TRUST IN NO MAN

TRUST IN NO MAN 2

TRUST IN NO MAN 3

BONDED BY BLOOD

SHORTY GOT A THUG

THUGS CRY

THUGS CRY 2

THUGS CRY 3

TRUST NO BITCH

TRUST NO BITCH 2

TRUST NO BITCH 3

TIL MY CASKET DROPS

RESTRAINING ORDER

RESTRAINING ORDER 2

IN LOVE WITH A CONVICT

LIFE OF A HOOD STAR

# Kingpen